Stories from Another World

ALSO BY SHEILA KOHLER

NOVELS

The Perfect Place
The House on R Street
Cracks
Children of Pithiviers

SHORT STORIES

Miracles in America
One Girl

Stories from Another World

SHEILA KOHLER

Ontario Review Press ✦ Princeton, NJ

Ontario Review Press
9 Honey Brook Drive
Princeton, NJ 08540

Distributed by W. W. Norton & Co.
500 Fifth Avenue
New York, NY 10110

Library of Congress Cataloging-in-Publication Data

Kohler, Sheila.
    Stories from another world / Sheila Kohler. — 1st ed.
      p. cm.
    ISBN 0-86538-110-0 (alk. paper)
     1. South Africa—Social life and customs—Fiction. 2. United States—
Social life and customs—Fiction. I. Title.

    PR9369.3.K64S76 2003
    823'.914—dc21

                                                      2003046288

First Edition

These stories have previously appeared in the following publications:
"Casualty," "Baboons," "All the Days of My Life" in *Ontario Review*; "Paris
by Night" in *Paris Review*; "Underworld," "Lunch with Mother"
in *Yale Review*; "The Mask" in *Bellevue Literary Magazine* and (in an
earlier version) in *Fiction*; "Death in Rome" in *The Antioch Review*; "Rain
Check" in *New Letters*; "The Adulterous Woman" in *Double Take*; "Youth" in
Five Points.

ACKNOWLEDGMENTS

I would like to thank those who read many of these stories, with discernment and benevolence: Blair Birmelin, Maureen Brady, Rebecca Kavaler, Sondra Olsen, Victoria Redel, Karen Satran, Christine Schutt, Susan Saiter, Terese Svoboda, Tim Tomlinson, and Gay Walley.

And for their important support, encouragement, example and friendship: Elizabeth Gaffney, Amy Homes, Francis Kiernan, Sandy McClatchy, Catherine Staley, Diane Williams, and Marnie Mueller.

My agent Robin Straus.

And once again to Amy Hempel my special thanks for the great gifts of her friendship and her boundless generosity and for continuing to be a writer's example in every way.

To my three wonderful girls: Sasha, Cybele, and Brett, thanks for love and guidance.

Once again this is for my beloved husband,
Bill,
my anchor and my sail

CONTENTS

Stories from Another World

Casualty

Through the trees in the mist she sees the hunters lined up
in the field with their little folding chairs and gray hats.
Somewhere, she knows, the beaters must be flushing out
the pheasants, forcing them up in the air. The French will,
apparently, do anything to shoot a bird. The birds, it seems to
her, do not have much of a sporting chance around here.

She is not supposed to walk about in the woods without a
gun in the hunting season, though she has a hunting permit
herself. Her husband, Michael, has taught her how to shoot.
But she walks on in blue jeans, a tight, black sweater, tennis
shoes, not the sort of clothes she used to wear. The change has
not gone unnoticed in this small French village.

She is supposed to be at home with her daughter, Cecily,
who is struggling with the French romantics. Every week she
has to learn a long poem by heart. This week it is the poem
about the death of Victor Hugo's child. Her daughter does
not have a good memory, or perhaps she has difficulty
concentrating. She opens windows, shuts them. She feels
drafts, she says. She is gloomy, then ecstatic. She walks around

in a sort of trance, as if she were listening to voices. She talks of strange twinges, flutters of the heart, but she would rather be out with her pony than learning poetry.

All summer long, the pony has followed Cecily around like a devoted dog on a long leash. She has built a house for him. She talks to him in a low secret voice. She talks more to her pony than she does to Sarah. She brushes him. His black coat has grown glossy from her brushing. He is docile, affectionate, a little stupid, perhaps, Sarah thinks, or anyway stubborn. He comes running in the early mornings when Cecily calls him; he nuzzles her neck, but if anyone tries to climb on his back, he rears up, bucks. The farmer says the pony is too old to train now; no one will ever ride him. She has warned Cecily not even to try. He will die wild, a wild pony.

Cecily, too, at fourteen, is restless. The wind makes her restless. The sound of the guns makes her restless. Her mother makes her restless. She is turning into a restless young woman with long legs and long arms. She is the one who dragged her mother on skis over the stones and ice of a closed ski path, the one who goes off for endless walks so that a policeman brought her back, believing she had run away. Sarah thinks her daughter is still in the living room, learning Victor Hugo by heart. She has told her daughter that she is going out for a breath of air.

Instead of turning back at the sight of the hunters, Sarah goes deeper into the woods. The November mornings are cold, but by now, late afternoon, she feels warmed by the exercise, the pale sunlight, the expectation. She likes these woods, these fields, the pale, cloud-flecked sky, the light yellow leaves, the mist. She remembers how she found the dog here once, his paw caught in a trap, and how she was obliged to press on the trap, driving the steel teeth deeper into the dog's paw, before she could release it. She remembers the dog's howls.

She sees a group of hunters walking toward her and recognizes Paul amongst them. It surprises her that she could be wandering around the woods in danger of being shot at, in the hope of a sighting of this man. She hears the sound of voices. Someone is saying something to Paul and he is responding, bending down and talking in a patient voice, explaining, instructing. He is talking to one of his boys.

Sarah likes his voice. She likes his patience with his children. Sarah, whose father died when she was seven, likes the way Paul Ravanel lays his hand very gently on his boys' heads. When she asks him about his children, he says he cannot wait to have them off his hands, but there is nothing he will not do for them, driving them around the countryside for soccer games, teaching them Latin grammar, mathematics. Sarah, too, has spent a lot of time with her children, but not with the diligence that Paul has. Even his children say they will not do for their children what he has done for them.

For a moment Sarah thinks the hunters are coming toward her, but they take another direction, and she returns to the house.

When she and her husband bought this house, an old mill in the Loiret, built over a shallow river, the agent told them it was called the *Moulin du Roi*. Afterward she found out that *Duruy* was just the name of the place. She has been living in the stone, creeper-covered house for years. There is a large garden where roses grow thick along the fence, and silver willows, not the weeping kind, line the banks of the river. Her daughter, Cecily, when she is not with her wild pony, canoes down the river or fishes with cotton and a bent pin, or sometimes she stands in the cold water and hunts for the tiny shellfish. This summer, it has not rained for a long time, and they have found dead fish like silver sequins scattered on the dry banks.

Sarah enters the familiar, cool hall with its worn black and white tiles, the low-beamed ceiling. The door to the cloakroom is ajar, so that she can see the tall white daisies through the window. For a moment she cannot see her daughter. Then she hears her voice, reciting. She is ensconced on the sofa with the water-lily pattern, her feet up on the coffee table in the living room reciting Victor Hugo.

Sarah thinks Cecily does not notice the flush in her mother's cheeks, the glitter in her eyes. Sarah does not know that Cecily has watched her mother walking down the driveway from the window, has followed her a way. She does not know, what she learns later, that the Portuguese maid, Fatima, who lives with her husband in the cottage, has also drawn aside her lace curtain and watched Sarah walking down the driveway from her small window. Sarah does not know that Fatima has sat on the end of Cecily's bed, when she had a cold, and asked the child if her mother has many lovers. Sarah does not know that Fatima has told all the other maids in the village who have told all the Madames in the village that the American Madame has many lovers.

Fatima is shocked by this, Madame's infidelity, but seems to take Monsieur's constant infidelity as natural. Fatima apparently accepts that Monsieur works in Paris, an hour from his home in the Loiret, that he passes his nights with his current mistress, a blond girl from Normandy who has a little scar down the side of her mouth which only makes her more attractive to him. Fatima accepts without comment, as Sarah does, that Monsieur only arrives here on weekends, driving fast across the courtyard, scattering the pebbles and then emerging slowly, dragging his long limbs out of the green Porsche.

Sarah is reckless and trustful, unaware of what people notice in the small village in the Loiret. She is a narrow-hipped and fine-boned woman, who has just turned forty. She has the outsider's high-pitched, loud laugh, the spoiled child's wide smile. Also, she has preserved an earnestness from her childhood, which her husband takes for stubbornness. "How can you be so stubborn?" her husband sometimes says to her, when he spends the weekend, his long limbs sprawled across the yellow deck chair by the river, sipping cider and eating *pâté en croute*, tilting his perfect profile to catch a wayward beam of French sun as it comes and goes behind cloud.

"How can you be so stupid?" is another thing Michael sometimes says to Sarah when she loses her keys. She is always losing things, forgetting the things Michael considers essential, like the mineral water he prefers: Perrier and not Badoit. But she doesn't think she is stupid. As a child she used to sign her letters, "From an undiscovered genius."

Sarah married very young, straight out of boarding school. She had two children, one of whom is already in college. She spends much of her time painting. She writes to her school friends, "At least I can hang them on my walls," referring to her unexhibited paintings. She has lived for many years abroad, on the edge of things.

Now she goes into the living room, turns on the lights. Outside the trees are merging with the mist. It is dusk, a time of melancholy. She draws the curtains. The walls are white and the rug and the sofa a soft blue. There is a corner cupboard that Michael found in a church that still smells of incense. The big fireplace is dark and empty.

The wind is still blowing. She hears the sound of the guns as she holds the book and listens to her daughter recite for the tenth time: *"Demain j'irai a l'aube."*

Sarah sits before the fire that night without closing the curtains, hoping to see what she eventually does: the lights of a car in the driveway. "I saw you in the woods today," she says to Paul when she lets him into the hall. He follows her into the kitchen, helps himself to some orange juice from the refrigerator, screws the top on the bottle tightly with one swift movement. She says in a lower voice, "Upstairs, in the bedroom. I'll be right up."

He lifts his eyebrows and nods. He knows the way. She goes into Cecily's small untidy room where her child lies, her blond hair spilled on the pillow, her covers tumbled on the floor. Sarah strokes the thick soft hair and leans closer to smell the familiar, slightly sour child smell.

Sarah remembers a moment in a butcher shop in Pithiviers when she propped her child up on the counter, a little girl with white curls and blue eyes in a white, smocked dress. While Sarah was hunting for her change, the stout, rosy-cheeked cashier stared at her child with longing and said, "I would give anything for a little girl like that."

Sarah covers her up, and the child opens her eyes and puts her arm around her mother's neck and draws her down. In the blue light she can see her own face in her daughter's: the slanting Tartar eyes, the high cheek bones, the straight nose. Unlike heroines in books, who are always prettier than they think they are, Sarah likes her face though her husband has told her once in a moment of candor, "You are not beautiful, but you have a likable face." Sarah particularly likes the reflection of her own aging face in Cecily's young one. She likes the plump hopeful cheeks, the glimmer of daring in her gray eyes. "Go to sleep, lovey," Sarah says, and the child closes her eyes obediently, seems to sleep. Sarah runs up the stairs into her bedroom. Paul is in the bathroom.

The bedroom is large and airy, open on one side to the driveway and on the other to the lawn with the river and the silver willows. She can see the moonlight in the leaves and the wild pony standing very still, as if waiting for something, on the edge of the field, a thick dark shadow. She hears the sound of the wind. She is afraid her daughter might wake, or even the maid, Fatima. What if Fatima's husband Jacqui, who takes care of the garden, were to rise to check on something? When she hears footsteps, the room swings around her, but it is Paul. He locks the door behind him and lights the bedside lamp.

For a moment she sees him as she first saw him outside the Japanese restaurant on the Rue de Berri, in movement. He seemed in a hurry as if he wanted to get the whole thing over fast, walking along the pavement with quick, small steps, talking fast, and waving his hands—a doctor, her friend had told her, she must meet him, what was sauce for the gander, etc., and so convenient with a property right near theirs in the Loiret, fortyish, a divorced man, father of three, with a heart murmur, perhaps, or something of that sort.

Probably he sees something similar as she stands before him, uncertain, afraid. Then as he steps into the room, the light is in his hair, his eyes. She is struck by the contrasts: the pale skin, the dark eyes, the dark eyebrows, the white hair. He looks young: a slight young man not much taller than she. His skin is smooth. There is something that seems to have protected his innocence like a shield, she thinks. He looks like a young man in a play with a white wig.

It begins as it always does: first the tenderness, the fun. She is no longer obliged, as she was in the early days with her husband, to pretend. There was the guilt of not feeling what she thought she was supposed to feel, the fraudulent sighs, copied from films, the still hips, the confessions of taking her pleasure alone.

She almost falls onto the floor when they fall together onto the narrow bed. And why has she not thought to wear something more attractive? The truth is she had not really believed that he would come, not tonight, not with her daughter in the house, the couple in the cottage which lies adjacent to the house.

He looks at her with hope, helplessly. He looked at her that way, the day in the fields. The first time this happened it was spring. They made love in the open fields, in the sunlight. She could hear the birds, the hum of a bee. They lay naked, tumbling around in the long grass, and afterwards Paul had a rash on his legs. She is moved by his slender body—the slight swell of his stomach, the broad, freckled back, the sweet, hopeful surge of his lust. She is moved by his need for her, as she imagines he is by hers. At the same time she is afraid that if he wants to do this now, he will not on Wednesday, when they usually meet at his office. She never knows if he will want to meet her again. He works long hours, finishes late with his patients. She brings him dinner in a basket which they eat hurriedly: stews, soups, apple compote, the kind of food her child likes to eat.

"Take your clothes off, please," he asks.

"We can't tonight. What if Cecily wakes?" Sarah says though she knows they will. They always do. They always leave the lamp lit so that she can see his body and her own. They have only done this once before in her house with her daughter present. That time, flailing around, Paul knocked a blue and white porcelain lamp onto the floor and broke it. Sarah did not have it repaired; she liked to look at the chip at the base. When her husband asked her what had happened, she said, "You know, I don't know how it happened. It must have been the wind."

There was no wind. The night they broke the lamp was a hot, still summer night. In the morning there was a storm. They were woken by the crack of thunder and the flash of lightning, and they made love. Sarah thinks of their love-making as electric, magic, and Paul the magician. Or sometimes she thinks he must take secret drugs to give her so much pleasure.

Now she says, "What about Fatima, Jacqui?"

He says, "The light was out in the cottage. They're asleep."

She takes all her clothes off, loses herself in their love-making. She feels as if she is flying free. Then she knows nothing else until she is woken by a loud knocking on the door.

She hears Fatima's voice calling hysterically, "Madame! Madame!"

Sarah says, "For God's sake, what on earth does the woman want?" The sun lies in a broad bar across the yellow carpet. She will remember it all her life.

"Ignore her, she'll go away," Paul says.

But the woman does not go away. Instead she goes on screaming, "Madame, Madame, come quickly, Cecily is dead!"

Cecily is not dead, but unconscious. Sarah and Michael sit side by side in silence on hard plastic chairs in the crowded waiting room of the hospital. They have been waiting all day in silence. Michael has said to Sarah, "How could you! In our bed! With the child in the house. What did you think would happen!"

Sarah said, "It was an accident."

Michael asked Paul to please have the decency to leave them alone with their child. Paul left the child with a colleague. He pressed her hand, rushed off down the corridor. Sarah will not see him on Wednesday night. Everything is different. A doctor has taken her child away.

Sarah wants to rush into the doctor's office and remind him they are still waiting, but she goes on sitting in the orange plastic chair between Michael and a potted plant with shiny leaves. She thinks of the wild black pony.

She rushed down the stairs in her dressing gown, followed by Paul, but it was too late. The pony was running wild, his tail flying. Cecily had somehow managed to mount him. For one triumphant moment she had ridden her pony across the field; then he had thrown her to the ground. She had fallen onto the stones beneath her. Jacqui held the child's head in his lap, his green jacket around her shoulders. Sarah knelt beside her, whispered her name. She seemed asleep.

Paul stooped over the child, felt the pulse. He said, "She is concussed. We must get her to the hospital." Sarah told Fatima to call Michael, to tell him what had happened, and Fatima told him at length what had happened. Michael arrived in his Porsche, his eyes red with weeping, his bottom lip wet and trembling.

Now the doctor emerges into the waiting room, beckons them to enter his small office. Sarah studies his glossy hair, the straight pink parting, with a sort of fascination. She can hardly concentrate on what he is saying, moving his small rosy mouth. His mouth is too small for his face, too delicate. He is showing them the X-rays. She thinks he has probably got the wrong X-rays. It must happen all the time in these crowded provincial hospitals. She has heard so many stories of test results proven false. He is pointing out the faint dark line of the fracture of the skull. How can that dark crack mark her child's young skull, and why is the doctor using the word skull, as though he were talking about a cadaver? He is telling them there has been some bleeding into the brain. It is not a very severe fracture and the bleeding is slight, but they will have to wait and watch the child. They should go and get something to eat and come back later that evening. There is nothing they can do now.

He is ushering them back into the waiting room, smiling, but shutting the door on them, leaving them with all the other gray people milling around in a sort of daze. A mother is pushing a drooling child in a wheelchair.

Sarah thinks she can smell Cecily's smell—that slightly sour child smell. She can feel her warm damp skin as she put her arms around her neck. She can feel the pressure of her hands on her neck. She can see the pale skin of her arms in the blue light. For some reason she remembers her as a little girl sitting in the bath and looking up at her mother and asking her, "What do I have to do to be popular, Mummy?" Sarah wants to hold the child's body pressed against hers, but it is Michael who puts his arm around Sarah's shoulder and says in a dry voice, "It won't help to weep. We ought to eat something. There must be some place to eat around here."

"I think there is a cafeteria in the basement," Sarah says mechanically and stops weeping.

They take a freight elevator down into the basement. The walls are green; the pipes visible. They pass a room where women are ironing sheets that makes Sarah think of a Cézanne painting, a stout woman putting her hand to her back, yawning. Sarah, too, feels exhausted, and at the same time as though she has stepped out of time. The sequence of things is jumbled in her mind, yet she knows they have been waiting all day for Cecily to wake up. Sarah's legs feel weak. Consciously she tries to breathe, to fill her lungs, to gulp in the air. She looks at her small white hands, her rings: her mother's hands, her mother's rings; the hands Cecily would have grown to have, the rings Cecily would have worn. Would have?

She thinks of making a pact with God or the devil: if her child lives she will give up her lover, Paul.

But she does not make a pact. Instead she eats the ham sandwich Michael brings her on the green plastic plate. She eats the salty white pickle, but all the time she sees Cecily looking up at her as she leant over her to kiss her good night, the blinded question in her gray eyes. Did she know Paul was in the house?

Michael says, "Go home and take a bath. I'll wait here until you get back. There is nothing you can do here. I'd rather be alone." But Sarah shakes her head. She wants to stay here. Michael sniffs slightly, his delicate nostrils arching like thin petals. "Take a bath for God's sake," he mutters. She blushes, lowers her eyes. He is right. She needs a bath, a long bath.

She emerges from the hospital and wanders around the parking lot. She has no memory of parking a car. She drives back to the house half blind. She does not remember where to turn. The ivy-covered house at the bottom of the hill looms suddenly into sight, the sun sinking behind it. She enters the cool, low-ceilinged hall. Fatima is waiting for her in the hall with a freshly baked pie, the laundry. Sarah wants to tell the woman to leave her alone, but she cannot because of the pie. Fatima in a crisis bakes; she wants to talk; she is distraught but also enjoying the drama of the situation, her position of power.

She says, "Oh, oh, Madame, Madame! I told her a million times not to try and ride that pony! How is she? What did the doctor say? What did Monsieur say?"

Sarah mumbles something vague, turns her back on the woman and goes to the foot of the stairs. They look steep, slippery, and the paintings of boxers in bellicose poses seem menacing to her. She wants to lie down on the bottom stair and sleep, but she drags herself upstairs, undresses, falls onto the bed.

Sarah hears the shutter in the bathroom banging and gets up to close it. She stands in the window and looks across the lawn. In the faint, early morning light she can see the leaves glisten and the pony standing very still at the edge of the field. Sarah goes downstairs, lifts the old ugly shotgun from the rack in the hall. It feels very heavy in her hand. She walks out into the fields, the long grass wet around her bare ankles.

The pony is still there standing at the edge of the field, as if waiting for someone. He is such a sturdy little thing, grown plump by then, his coat shiny in the early morning light. The breeze flattens the grass and stirs his dark mane. He lifts his head as she comes nearer, staring at her, but he does not move at all except for a faint twitching up and down his dark back and a swish of his tail. She approaches. He shakes his head, tosses his mane, whinnies at her, as if there were something he wanted to say, as if he knows her, remembers, perhaps, the carrots she brought him, the lumps of sugar, or her smell. She remembers the dark pony running free, its tail flying, and the blond hair spread on Jacqui's knee. He trots nearer. Then she lifts the shotgun and works the bolt on the old thing and her hands are trembling and her mouth is dry.

Paris by Night

S he surveys the room where she has slept all the eighteen
years of her life: the old brass bed, the pink armchair in the
corner where she has read so many books, the Queen Anne
tallboy where she has kept her sweaters and her secrets—the
diary where she recorded what she did and the one where
she wrote down her fantasies, which her mother discovered
and believed to be real. Questioned about it, Maureen told
her mother it was all made up. "I'm glad to hear it! The
thought of your doing something of that kind!" her mother
said, referring, Maureen presumes, to the nude swims in
the dark, dangerous water of the Indian ocean with a
mysterious stranger.

She checks the drawers of the tallboy to make sure she has
packed everything. Her embroidered silk underwear with the
new monogram, her white lace night-dress for the wedding
night, her chiffon dresses, her patent leather pumps, and her
seed pearls lie neatly in the maroon suitcase with its nylon
lining on the table under the window.

She has promised her mother she will go to bed early tonight to prepare for what her mother calls the Big Day, but she wants to take a drive into the city for the last time in her unmarried life. She tiptoes past her mother's room, down the carpeted stairs and through the hall, past the big bouquet of peonies in the tureen, and steps out the Dutch door. She stands a moment in the hot garden, now quiet as a cemetery, and looks back at the white gabled house. She breathes in the smell of freshly cut grass and roses and compost, as though she has never done it before. She feels a weight on her heart. She is wide open to the rooks caw cawing, to the gold light, to the brightness in the air, to the solemn hush, the strange, dream-like clarity of the outlines of things.

She climbs into the leather seat of the long low sports car, another of her mother's wedding gifts to the young couple. The car salesman had stroked its shiny black bonnet with a grin and said to her fiancé, "Watch out for this leopard." Dave likes to drive fast cars.

He will be getting dead drunk with his tennis-playing friends at his bachelor party. Her mother, thank goodness, will be eating her supper on a tray in her room, her face plastered with mask.

Maureen searches for the car keys through the confusion of objects in her heavy handbag, making the little charms on her bracelet jingle: the tickets for Paris, the traveler's checks, the passport. She has left the keys on the dresser in her room. She is always forgetting or misplacing things. She leaves the handbag on the seat of the car and tiptoes back up the stairs past her mother's room. She thinks of her mother saying, "It is services, not love, that makes a marriage last," though her mother's marriage did not last, ending after only a few years with her husband's heart attack, a man much older than she, whose money assured that she would not have to perform services for anyone else.

Maureen thinks of the services she has performed for her mother over the years: the parties she has attended, dragging herself away from her books, standing alone on the dance floor in a tight dress and fixing some young man in the eye so that he could not refuse. Her mother has required her to be *popular*, not an unreasonable requirement, after all, but one she has had to work as hard at as though she were learning Sanskrit.

With her keys in hand, she throws her handbag onto the car floor and struggles with the unfamiliar stick shift. She can never get the damned thing into reverse. She takes off with a lurch and descends the steep road. She likes to drive alone through the blue hills in the evening light, the window open, the steamy air on her face, the flat flamboyants, with their wild red flowers, flashing past her like paradise. She presses on the accelerator, speeding toward the city that lies below her in the valley by the sea.

In the glare of gold evening light she sees a man step off the curb at the corner, coming toward her. She reaches over to lock her door and wind up her window fast. She should not have come this way. The neighborhood is not safe, and the traffic, terrible. She is obliged to stop at the red light, and the man has his hands splayed against her window. He pushes his face up against the glass, his mouth open, shouting something at her angrily. He is rocking her car. She waits for the light to turn, keeping her gaze on the road, her hands sweating, her mouth dry. She takes off with a screech of rubber against the road, looks back, and sees the man stumble away, his head down. She turns on the radio, her hands shaking. The newscaster announces a bus strike.

She looks in her rear-view mirror. The poor man is wandering slowly across a field. She thinks she has acted like a silly child. She has been selfish, unfeeling, she should have picked him up. He had not wished her harm, after all. He has been walking a long way; he is exhausted, desperate, perhaps. He has a sick wife, or child waiting for him at home.

She winds down the window, unlocks the door, hums along with the music: "Don't be cruel to a heart that's true. I don't want no other love."

She thinks of the mounds of white tulle, hanging on the back of her bedroom door, with the orange blossom tiara slung over one satin shoulder and the white satin shoes placed neatly side by side below. Her head spins at the thought of so much whiteness.

Her mother has insisted on a formal wedding with a white tulle dress, though Maureen is already several weeks pregnant. Her mother has told her firmly, "It has to be white, darling. You must think of the guests who are coming from all over the place; they expect a good show, after all."

So a good show has been planned: the lily-of-the-valley to be clutched in her manicured hands; her heavy hair to be swept up and scraped back from her face in an elaborate chignon, which pulls at the sides of her forehead and makes her cheeks look even plumper, but allows the orange blossoms to be placed like a trembling crown on her head; the reception, to be conducted under the yellow awning on the freshly mowed grass, with the smoked salmon and the *foie gras* and the French champagne; the bride and groom to be caught in photographs standing on the stone arch over the fish pond so that their wavy, black-and-white reflections show up in the dark water; her dead grandmother's priceless, blue diamond ring, said to bring bad luck—

"something borrowed something blue," her mother has told Dave—to be worn as an engagement ring; the honeymoon in a famous hotel in Paris with tickets to the opera and an evening at the Moulin Rouge, to be paid for by the mother of the bride.

"Don't be cruel to a heart that's true. I don't want no other love."

Someone is waiting on the curb at the next light. He raises his thumb, and she draws over. The glare is in her eyes, and she shades them but can hardly make out the man's face. He speaks with a slight accent—Russian perhaps or some other Eastern European language, a dark wing of hair falling over his low forehead. He says something she does not quite catch. "What is it?" she asks and turns off the radio. He inquires where she is heading, and she tells him she is just driving and instantly regrets it. She should have invented a destination.

She notices the thrust of slim hips against the car door. "May I?" he asks politely, his hand on the door handle. She hesitates a moment, notices his long legs in khaki trousers, slightly stained around the edges, a T-shirt with a faded image of an airplane, or perhaps it's a boat. She nods her head, and he opens the door, settles himself in the seat, stretches out, slamming the door hard behind him. There is something cat-like, predatory about his movements that makes her heart hammer so hard the car seems to shimmy. Perspiration pricks her underarms.

"Nice car," he says and touches the smooth wooden dashboard, his fingers lingering proprietorially.

She shifts her gaze to the congested road, but she can smell him. His odor fills the car, something slightly musty mixed with smoke and sweat, a strong animal smell. When she does glance at him, she sees the blue shadow under the pale skin and thinks he is someone who has not seen sunlight recently—probably a criminal, someone who has escaped from prison, perhaps someone who will slit her throat.

And he is not even very young: she notices the gray in the dark hair, a hard line that runs from his nostril to the side of his wide mouth. Big hands hold his long thighs. He does not attempt to make conversation, surely the duty of any legitimate hitchhiker.

She considers asking him to get out, but before she can do so, he lifts his narrow hips slightly to pull a crumpled packet of cigarettes from the pocket of his tight trousers. She hears the rustle in his hands. He offers her a cigarette. She is about to say she does not smoke, but he slips the cigarette into her hand. He pushes in the car lighter and slings his arm around the back of her seat. They smoke, sweating in the lingering heat which rises from the tarmac. They are trapped in traffic, the cars inching forward as if in slow motion.

Why is Dave not here at her side? Bachelor parties are absurd. Dave had not even wanted to go to his, or so he told her. He doesn't like to drink. Alcohol gives him a headache. There was some talk of hiring a hooker, something Dave maintained he would have found extremely distasteful. He confessed that his first sexual experience was with a woman of this kind, and that the sight of her, washing herself in preparation for the act, had so filled him with disgust he had had great difficulty going through with it.

Her mother expected her to marry someone eligible, but she fell pregnant, miraculously pregnant, after the first time she ever did it, with Dave. How could she possibly have refused him, after he had dragged her all the way up the *koppie*, the blackjacks catching in his socks? He had shown such dogged determination, struggled so valiantly with her tight clothing,

19

fumbled around for simply ages, trying to unlatch her brassiere, and desperately dragging her clinging girdle down to her knees, as though his life depended on it, and all in the dark on a rock at the school dance.

Besides, all the girls want to do it with Dave, because he is an aggressive tennis player with a terrific serve who does very well at exams although he only studies the night before, sitting up and reading the books everyone else has had to study for months. Dave is smart and quick. All the girls want to do it with him because he is a tall, loose-limbed, blond adolescent, who is always lucky, wins at poker, and wears V-necked white sweaters with a border of maroon and navy blue, hand knitted by his adoring, widowed mother who works as a secretary at his school in order to pay for her son's tuition. Though dirt poor, Dave has declared that he will be a millionaire before he is thirty.

She remembers shopping with her mother and Dave in a small, dark antique shop. Dave picked up a Spanish fan and spread it slowly to show her the pretty, pink flowers. She lifted it to her face and fanned herself. He said he wished he could buy it for his mother. Her mother offered to buy it for him. Dave blinked his white tipped eyelashes, and his bottom lip protruded, trembling. He hung his small, blond head as he said, "I feel so awful, having no money at all." Her short mother reached up and gathered the tall fellow into her arms.

She is coming to the fork in the road which leads either into the center of the city, or toward the beach. She glances at the stranger inquiringly. He indicates the road toward the beach. It is not late. The light still streams, mote-flecked and gold, through the shade trees on the sides of the road. She likes to see the sun sink fast below the sea, to feel the cool sea wind, to hear the waves break with a crash on the sand. She has always liked the wild, mysterious sea along this southern coast. She watches him stub out his cigarette in her ashtray, the tips of his fingers yellow, the nails unclean. He leans back in his seat, crosses his arms, closes his dark eyes. She notices the broad shoulders, the long, almost delicate neck, the way his head falls back and slightly to one side, which makes her think of a painting of a saint by an Italian painter she has seen in a book.

The thought crosses her mind: "I don't want to see the girls do the cancan at the Moulin Rouge." She remembers going to Paris with her mother, and how her mother had insisted they take a bus trip to see Paris by Night. They went from one strip joint to the next, drinking more at each one. She thought it might be the same strippers, scarves tied over their heads, muffled in coats, who slipped surreptitiously into the dark of the back of the bus, giggling and whispering, following her and her mother from one place to the next, emerging each time under the lights in a new outfit which they proceeded to remove bit by bit, exposing the same tired, gray flesh. She said to her mother, "But I could just have looked at myself in the mirror and seen something better than that!"

"But that wouldn't have been art," her mother said.

"And you think this is?" she said.

She takes the road toward the sea. The man is sitting quietly beside her now, not looking at her, his head nodding slightly. Perhaps he is actually asleep, exhausted by escaping from the police? From his wife of many years, his screaming children?

She thinks of her baby whose presence within her body seems as unreal as the night nude swims with the stranger she once invented in her diary of fantasies. She has not felt nauseated; in fact, she has never felt as well. Only the cessation of the monthly flow and the satisfying swell of her breasts have announced the baby's presence. She remembers the doctor frowning with disapproval and saying, "And now just what do you think you are going to do about this?"

"Get married," she said airily, as though she were talking about going to the bank. It did not cross her mind to do anything else. And had anything else ever crossed Dave's mind, she wonders now. Was that why he had dragged her up the *koppie* with such determination?

She stops at the edge of the beach and looks across the sand at the dark sea which folds away into the darkening sky. There is no one on the long twilit beach. Huge waves rise up and break with a crash on the shore. The sea wind shakes the feathery leaves of the cassias and the fringe of monkey ropes and jungle root.

She looks at the stranger. He remains so still, his eyes shut, that for a moment she thinks he might be dead. She leans toward him to study his thin face and arched nose, the close-set eyes. She listens to the even breathing. She inhales his breath. She considers waking him.

She remembers how her lonely mother, on holiday in the summer, on the hot nights in hotel rooms, would wake her. "Keep me company, will you, darling, I feel so blue," her mother would say, lifting the sheet of her bed. She would rise obediently and stumble across the big empty room and climb up into the bed beside her mother's hot, sweating body. Her mother would stroke her hair and murmur, "My baby, my little one," and she would think, "Some little one!" pressing her plump thighs together to pleasure herself, imagining the swish of the skirts of nuns in their black habits, walking with little whips within walled gardens.

She slips off her sandals and drops them on the floor beside her handbag. She leaves the keys in the ignition and the car door open, stepping out onto the warm tarmac. She runs quickly across it to the soft, hot sand, going down to the edge of the wild sea. Wrathful waves pound the shore. They crash against the rocks with such force that the spray rises high and then collapses, descends, races down the rocky planes. She looks across the dark water, watching a bold ruby sun sink below the horizon.

She hears the clack of her car door, the muffled metallic sound of the engine. Music is instantly blaring. She spins around to see the shiny black car draw slowly away from the beach. It seems to her in the glare of gold light that the stranger is waving to her and smiling. It occurs to her to run toward him, to scream wildly, "Come back! come back!" but she would never be able to catch up with him.

She turns her back on the road and the blue hills where her home lies with a feeling close to relief. Possibilities blossom. It occurs to her that she is still free, untrammeled, unwed. She does not have to wear her dead grandmother's priceless blue diamond ring, said to bring bad luck. She does not have to stay at the famous hotel in Paris. She does not have to go to the opera. She does not even have to marry Dave. She imagines herself and her baby on their own in some foreign port. She sees herself pushing a pram along a French pier. The wind is blowing the spray into her face.

She looks along the deserted beach, and then at the water which glints invitingly, cool and dark. It shimmers like *crepe de Chine*, a pinkish brown in the twilight. She does what she has always wanted to do in this savage place where swimming is not permitted because of the strong currents, the big breakers:

she strips off her shirt, her pleated skirt, her underwear, and leaves them in a pool at her feet. She runs naked, in only her charm bracelet. She goes across the sand and plunges into the wild water. She is a strong swimmer and dives easily under one wave after the other, stretching out her arms, kicking up a rainbow spray, reaching for the horizon, striking out for a new world.

Underworld

This Sunday I watch silently while the rest of the girls go off down the school driveway in their Sunday-white dresses, the mother-of-pearl buttons gleaming in the light, their Panama hats on the back of their heads. They wave to me or shout, "Hard luck," going home to be stuffed with food by their mothers, to loll by their swimming pools, or giggle helplessly in the sunlight on the tennis court. I sit in the shade on the wooden bench in my brown tunic. My thick blond hair is tightly plaited down my back, and I swing my heavy brown lace-ups back and forth defiantly.

I am eleven years old, in disgrace, though I do not consider what I have done disgraceful, cannot even conceive that anything I might do would be disgraceful.

I have the impression of entering a dream: an eerie silence hangs in the low, wisteria-covered pergola, and a strange stillness settles over the terraced garden. The sunlight on the white gables blinds me, and the giant shadows cast by the tamarinds release great waves of soft green perfume, but under the perfume I detect a darker smell. Mademoiselle, the

French teacher, who is left to guard me in my disgrace, sits beside me, a shawl around her shoulders, despite the heat. She holds herself erect, like a sentinel.

My mother has complained that it is bad enough that the school should deprive her of her darling daughter's presence on one of the few days she is allowed to go home, but to leave her with the French teacher, when everyone knows that some scandal is attached to her name! "What's an Italian princess doing out there in the middle of nowhere, teaching French, I ask you?" Mother has muttered to me. I replied that Mademoiselle was of the Roman nobility, but had had a French governess as a child and had spent many years in France. I did not mention that she had told us to shut the windows so that she could gossip about the other teachers, or that we were to tell her when we had our periods for the first time.

Now Mademoiselle leans toward me to speak in her deeply accented voice, and I draw back from her and hold my breath.

She says that she has no wish to punish me more than I have already been punished. Her sallow skin glints green in the sunlight, and her white hair rises above her square face like a fan. Perspiration dots the deep shadow on her upper lip. She rises and tells me to follow her and walks ahead of me. She is barrel-shaped: short and stout with thin, brittle ankles. She wears high heels and carries herself upright. As I follow slowly, at some distance, I can hear the sad sigh of her stockings rubbing against her stout thighs and smell her odor which trails like the train of a gown.

She ushers me into the book-lined library with its blood-red carpet and its velvet curtains closed on the Southern sunlight. She stands for a moment in the deep silence, considering. She chooses a thick volume, bound in leather, gives it to me and sends me down into the bottom of the garden. "It will be cool and shady down there, dear," Mademoiselle says not unkindly, and gives me the heavy book which she tells me I will surely enjoy.

I run through the rose garden, under the tamarinds, and down the stone steps, skipping two at a time. I sink down in the deep shade of an oak tree. On the first page of the book, a black Greek chariot, drawn by black horses with wings on their shoulders, descends, going toward the center of the earth. I read, and indeed the myths take me to another place. I particularly like the story of Persephone, carried away by the God of the underworld. I read on and on until I hear a deep voice calling me. I look up, dazzled by the light, and see Mademoiselle, a thick, squat shadow, standing on the wisteria-covered terrace, her hand shading her eyes. She is calling me for lunch.

Lunch is served in the long, paneled dining room. Bereft of the girls' constant chatter and the clatter of china, the place seems strange and dim and dusty. And there is Mademoiselle's stagnant smell, beneath that of the food. The food is worse than usual. It is impossible to guess what kind of beast the sullen servant serves us. He, too, has to work this Sunday because of my disgrace. We eat something mysteriously dark and leathery and suffocated in a thick black sauce. I push my food around my plate, but Mademoiselle chews doggedly, eating painfully slowly, earnestly, holding each morsel in the side of her mouth, as though loathe to relinquish it. A bead of moisture dangles from her arched nostril, and her high forehead glints in the gloom.

An ominous silence hangs in the long dining room. The high commissioner stares down at us through his monocle from his portrait on the wall. Perhaps Mademoiselle does not consider it fitting to speak to me—after all, I am supposed to be in disgrace. Or perhaps she is thinking of other things.

The servant announces that there will be no dessert, and I am surprised to see a look of pain pass across Mademoiselle's face. She puts her little fat fingers to her forehead delicately and draws her lips into a thin line and says something which sounds rude in Italian. "Very well," she says to the servant.

Finally we rise. Mademoiselle bows her head and says, "For what we have received may the Lord make us truly thankful." She looks at me with a glint of irony in her gray eyes. She hesitates. The long hot afternoon stretches before us dully. I shift my weight from one foot to the other and chew the side of my cheek, and think of the juicy roast beef, the crispy Yorkshire pudding, the fresh fruit salad and ice cream Mother always serves me on Sundays. I think of the sparkling pool, the white parasol turning in the wind, the sweet scent of honeysuckle that grows wild along the hedge.

I want to suggest Mademoiselle send me back to my book in the garden. Instead, she says, "It is very hot. We will rest inside for a while." I am about to climb the stairs, to go to my dormitory with my book, when she calls me back. "Come with me. It is cooler downstairs." I am obliged to follow her down to the staff rooms, a region I have never visited before. I am surprised by the smallness and darkness of her room. It appears even smaller because it is crowded with heavy furniture with claws for feet and silver-backed brushes and combs, little pots and embroidered doilies and old photos in black frames. There is a crucifix, blood running from the hands and feet, on the wall.

A window gives onto the garden, but it is closed, and the creeper has grown so thickly over the ledge, its tendrils clinging to the bars, it obscures the light. Perhaps Mademoiselle notices the expression on my face because she gives me a glance of sad complicity and says, "She gave me the worst room, of course, the smallest. You should see *hers*," referring, I understand, to our headmistress, Miss Temple, a young, blond woman with an M.A. from Oxford.

She tells me to sit down in the only chair in the room, a brown, leather armchair in the corner. I obey, sitting pressed as far back as possible, trying to breath lightly, fast, taking in little sips of air, so that my head spins and adds to the strangeness of the room which comes to me as in a dream, distanced, muffled, alien.

She sits down on the bed, crosses her legs, wafting her terrible odor through the room. She says she is very sorry I have been kept in on such a lovely Sunday, and she looks longingly out the window and sighs deeply.

I say, "I'm sorry you have to stay in school, too."

She smiles and shrugs and says it does not matter. "To tell you the truth, I was the one who asked to stay in with you. I have nowhere else to go," she admits, and her sallow skin looks gray, and I realize she is even older than I thought. A mournful silence pervades. I try to think of something cheerful to say.

She puts her small elegantly shod feet side by side, leans toward me, her fleshy elbows on her knees. I press back in my chair. She tells me she feels toward me as she would have toward one of her own family. She has no family left at all. They are all dead, she says. "You cannot imagine how far away, distant, I feel, from all of this," she confesses and waves her fingers around the room.

She tells me she has had a difficult life. She almost died several times. She says that she was captured by the Nazis during the war. She was tortured. They pulled out her fingernails. They put her in baths of freezing and then boiling hot water, so that she fainted and fainted again. The women, she maintains, were much braver than the men. "I didn't know anything to tell them, but even if I had, I would not have said a word," she says and looks at me, considering. "I wager *you* can keep a secret," she says and smiles at me.

I am not sure what to say to all of this but stare about me in a sort of trance. I can hardly breathe in the closeness of the room, Mademoiselle's presence. Increasingly a dim haze is cast over everything. What can I do but nod my head?

She says she wants to show me something she has never shown anyone else. She would never show anyone else but me, because she feels, instinctively, I will understand, will be able to keep the secret. "You are like me. We are one of a kind," she says, her gray eyes turning bright as she lifts two fingers and crosses them in a gesture that seems almost obscene to me. "You, too, are different from the rest. I realized that when I heard the way you spoke up to her. None of the others would have dared to speak like that to Miss Temple. You, too, are a rebel like me and brave. You are alone like me, but you don't care, do you?" she asks me in a low passionate whisper. She leans closer, talking about my outburst to the headmistress, the angry words that have caused my disgrace.

I huddle back in my chair trying not to breathe. I want to cry out, *No, no, I am not like you! I will never be like you! I don't want to be alone, an unloved spinster. I will never be old and I will never smell like you do.* But I nod again.

"Who would I show it to if not you, who understands me?" she says. Of all the girls in the school, I am the only one to be so privileged. She looks at me, and her gray eyes glitter fervently.

"I understand," I say and stare at her. I cannot but stare at her, fascinated as one might be by a boa swallowing a chicken in the zoo.

Have I ever seen a French foundation garment, she asks me. I am not quite sure what she is talking about and can only think to open my mouth a little and look at her with horror and say, "Oh, no, never!"

She proceeds to have me help her with the small buttons on the back of her dress. I am obliged to stand close beside her and to unfasten all the tiny, difficult, cloth-covered buttons, one by one. I fumble in my haste, afraid to touch her clammy body, redolent with her repellent odor. She takes off her dress, and the smell of her exposed flesh fills the small room. I am obliged to sit down again, my head spinning.

She stands in the light by the window and says in a lilting voice, "You see how lovely it is." I stare.

The article is a most intricate, strapless garment made, she points out, of cream lace, whalebone, and white elastic. She shows me the advantages, moving her little hands gracefully and unleashing waves of dank odor. "See how it's padded for extra fullness, here,"she says, as she smoothes her hands lovingly over the bodice, where her flesh spills over the top. "A girl's waist," she declares as she puts both hands on the wide waist, elbows out, fingers splayed. "A little liberty here," she concedes, stroking the spread of the hips. Then, and most dreadfully, she snaps the elastic of a suspender coquettishly to show me the small blue stars that are studded all along the fat leg. I am breathless, dizzy, the room spins about me. I hold onto the arms of my chair.

I become aware she is waiting for some sort of response, head poised expectantly. I am unable to speak. "I see," is all I can whisper, and when that is not enough, obviously, I manage to add, "That's nice, yes, lovely."

"I bought it in Paris when I was there last. The older I get the more I think a foundation garment is important," she tells me as though imparting some most essential advice. She declares, tilting her double chin bravely, "I would rather go without food than a foundation garment." She says with a sigh, "I'm afraid I realized it too late. I let too many opportunities slip through my fingers, and now I am alone."

She stands very straight and turns slightly so that I can admire all of it, and so that her odor grows stronger in the room, and I cannot help but notice the dark secret source of the smell, and how her ancient flesh sags between the legs, as though it were not part of her but has fallen away, some useless covering she would gladly shed. She stares down at her terrible wasted flesh. "For me its too late, you understand, but for you, there is still time," she says urgently and sits down on the bed, very near me, and takes both my hands into hers and stares into my eyes. I draw back from her damp, hot grasp in terror. I cannot breathe, overwhelmed by the smell of rot. I rise and run from the room. I catch a glimpse of her as I go through the door slumped over slightly, folding her arms along the whalebone against her chest, staring before her.

I run up the stairs to the dormitory. I go into the bathroom at the end of the long silent corridor and wash my hands, my face. I stand before the mirror and stare at my face, the water running down my cheeks. My skin looks green, my eyes glitter strangely, my lips look thin and chapped. The air is still redolent with Mademoiselle's odor, as though she has followed me up the stairs. I look around me, but no one is there. I lift my arm, and smell my skin. I become aware of the source of the terrible odor. It comes from my body. It has always been there under the sweet scent of flowers.

The Mask

T hey asked him to come as soon as possible to discuss a case: a patient who ate things—plastic forks, paper clips, Styrofoam cups, anything he could lay his hands on; apparently he did not discriminate. He had been doing this for years, they said, or so the young psychiatrist understood, from the somewhat garbled telephone conversation with a doctor with a heavy Eastern European accent, who called from some place upstate.

The young psychiatrist called an older colleague for his opinion. The colleague said he had heard of things of this sort, but rarely. He said he was not certain that the diagnosis was the right one.

The psychiatrist took the train. The railroad followed the river for a while, but he did not look up from the article he was writing. He hardly noticed the gray water or the rain falling against the dirty windows. When he did glance up, he saw flat fields spread out on either side. It was late afternoon when he arrived at the small station. The sky was clearing, the light intense. The glare made him shield his eyes. It was very quiet up there with only woods and fields around him. A dog barked in the distance.

He stood alone on the platform for a moment and shivered. It was early spring but colder up here. The emptiness of the place, the silence, the evening glare made him feel exposed. He had lived all his life in big cities and thought of the country as a place without culture, the people prejudiced, ignorant, and dull. Nothing would induce him to live in a place like this, he thought.

The doctor in charge of the hospital, a stout elderly man with luxuriant white hair and thick glasses, was waiting for him on the steps of the waiting room. With his striped tie blown over his shoulder, the doctor stared at the psychiatrist, uncertainly. The psychiatrist smiled, introduced himself, and explained that everyone thought he was too young to be a psychiatrist. He did not tell the elderly doctor that he had had to do his studies in a hurry, had done his undergraduate degree in three years at Harvard, his doctor's degree in four. He knew he had a boyish air with his thick reddish hair, large brown eyes, and smooth skin that was often taken for innocence.

The elderly doctor seemed flustered, dropped some papers on the floor, and could hardly bring himself to shake the psychiatrist's hand. He said, "So *good* of you to come all this way," and inclined his head deferentially.

They drove along a rutted road in the elderly doctor's battered car. The road narrowed and dipped a little. They crossed a small bridge that needed a coat of paint. The elderly doctor pointed out the institution through the car's window as they approached. In the distance, rising up through the trees, the psychiatrist saw the building. It had been a grand hotel or a mansion at one time, the elderly doctor told the psychiatrist proudly. It was a nineteenth-century edifice in a state of disrepair, with a sort of porch with Greek columns, the white paint flaking, and woods on either side.

The elderly doctor ushered the psychiatrist down a long green corridor into a conference room. A bare yellow bulb hung from the ceiling over a table covered with green baize. The varnished floor glistened. For a moment the psychiatrist thought of Van Gogh. He had had a passion for paintings as a boy but had given up his studies of art to become a psychiatrist.

Several faces were lifted toward him. Introductions were made. There was a psychologist, a thin woman no longer young, with a string of bright, green beads around her scrawny neck; an internist who came from the Philippines; some Indian residents; an Irish intern. The psychologist immediately embarked on a long history of the patient in an unexpectedly deep voice, twisting her green beads around her fingers nervously, as she told the psychiatrist what seemed to him trivial and tiresome details about the patient's life, about the patient's mother, about his violent father who had shot the patient's girlfriend's father and was now in jail. From her remarks the psychiatrist learned only that the patient had been hospitalized for most of his life; several experts had been consulted; he had received various treatments, none of which had had any effect; and the previous week he had once again eaten a plastic fork, had been operated on, and had almost died.

"The condition seems to be chronic," the psychologist said and twisted her green beads tightly around her neck.

The doctor in charge sighed, adjusted his glasses, and said, "Everything possible has been done for the poor man, but nothing makes any difference."

The young psychiatrist felt bored and hungry. He remembered he had not had time for lunch. He asked if it would be possible to have a cup of tea. Someone brought him one, which he drank fast, slopping the tea into the saucer. He wished someone would offer him something to eat. A vision of a large bowl of popcorn rose up in his mind.

He became aware that the psychologist was saying, "After he's worn it for a while, the behavior stops—temporarily, at least."

The psychiatrist thought of something. "Did someone say the man suffers from asthma?" he asked suddenly. They all nodded cheerfully. The psychiatrist nodded back, looked around at the faces, and noticed the Philippine internist smiling at him, genially. Someone else, one of the Indian residents perhaps, said, "It has proved most effective, when the man can be brought to wear it."

Out of the corner of his eye, he caught sight of something dark on the table. For a moment he thought of a small child wearing the thing so as not to hurt his head when it was banged against a wall. He asked if he could see it. Someone passed it to him. He held it in his hands, turned it around. There were two slits for the eyes and a small opening for the nose and tiny perforations where it covered the cheeks as if to allow the beard to grow through.

The psychiatrist asked to see the patient. The doctor in charge suggested one of the male nurses remain in the room.

The psychiatrist said, "I don't think that will be necessary," but thought of another patient he had once treated, a rich Arab, who had taken a bite out of his cheek. He said, "Well, let him stand behind the door."

A male nurse brought the patient into the room. The nurse left and locked the door from the outside but remained looking through the glass panel at the top of the door.

The psychiatrist introduced himself and shook the patient's hand, a large, red hand. The patient grasped his hand firmly and asked, "Dr. Wren? Don't I know you from somewhere?"

The psychiatrist smiled and shook his head, though for a second he did think there was something familiar about the patient. He was a tall, loose-limbed fellow with reddish hair and a small scar on his upper lip.

They sat down facing one another across the wide table. The psychiatrist asked the patient about his life in this place.

The patient leaned toward the psychiatrist and looked at him with intelligent, dark-brown eyes. He looked as though he wanted to tell the psychiatrist—and him alone—something important, but he said nothing.

After a while, the psychiatrist asked, "How do you feel?"

The patient said suddenly, "You have to do something for me!"

The psychiatrist nodded and smiled. "I will try."

He gave the patient a piece of paper and a pencil and asked the man to draw the face of a clock and set the hands pointing to ten minutes to three.

The patient asked, "Why are your hands shaking?"

The psychiatrist stretched forth his large long-fingered hands and looked at them. He laughed, "Too much caffeine."

The patient drew all the numbers of the clock bunched up into one quadrant. The psychiatrist looked at the drawing carefully and then at the patient's face for a moment. "Try it again," the psychiatrist urged, but the patient drew the same thing. Then the psychiatrist frowned and took out his address book, a paper clip, and a pen from his pocket and placed them on the edge of the table before him. He

37

told the patient to look at the three objects and to try to remember them.

The patient reached out suddenly for the paper clip, but the psychiatrist caught his hand in time and shook his head. "Just look," he said and turned his head slightly to one side and smiled.

The patient said, "I promise I'll never do anything like that again," and turned and looked over his shoulder toward the window, where the male nurse stood watching. The psychiatrist urged the patient to study the objects in order to remember them. The patient stared at the objects for a moment. Then the psychiatrist slipped the objects into his pocket. He asked the patient if he could name them. The patient shook his head impatiently and leaned closer to the psychiatrist and whispered, "All I want is to leave this place. Can you imagine what it's like in a place like this, being watched all the time?" Again he glanced at the nurse.

The psychiatrist asked the patient if he was sure he could not remember any of the objects shown to him, but the patient only rose from his chair and walked over to a window. He stood with his back to the young psychiatrist, looking out the window, his large, red hands lifted to either side of his head and pressed against the pane of glass. The psychiatrist, too, rose and looked out another window at the rain that had begun to fall again. He noticed the thick silver drops falling obliquely, caught in the lamplight like ash. All around the place were open fields. It was farming country now, though once, the psychiatrist thought, there had probably been elegant estates along the river.

The psychiatrist thought of something else. There was something he wanted to know, he said, a question he wanted to ask. Haltingly, he asked the man if he was drawn to some things more than others. The patient turned slowly and seemed to be considering the psychiatrist. He had the impression that the patient was about to speak frankly to him. Then he walked toward the psychiatrist and stood beside him, with something like collusion in his eyes. The patient smiled slightly as he said, "I try to find things that fit my personality."

The psychiatrist shuddered and felt his heart begin to flutter irregularly.

The patient moved closer to him, standing right beside him, so that the psychiatrist realized the patient was about the same height as he was. The patient came even closer and whispered in his ear, "They watch me, or they make me wear the mask." The psychiatrist stared at him and noticed a despairing and agitated expression in his eyes. The patient glanced over his shoulder and jerked his head toward the male nurse. The psychiatrist waved the nurse away from the window. The nurse hesitated and raised his eyebrows inquiringly. The psychiatrist made an impatient gesture, and the nurse stepped away from the window. The psychiatrist could hear him talking to someone in the corridor in Spanish. The staccato Spanish words, which the psychiatrist did not understand, sounded loud and angry.

The psychiatrist sat down and gestured to the patient to do the same. He leaned toward him and said in a low voice, "I think I may be able to help you." The patient's eyes turned bright. The psychiatrist asked if anyone had given him these tests before. The patient said, "Tests?"

The psychiatrist raised his eyebrows and shook his head. He said, "It is possible you may be able to leave this place."

"When?" the patient asked, staring at the psychiatrist, his eyes glittering. He began walking back and forth across the small room restlessly, as though hunting for something. The psychiatrist could hear the sound of the patient's shoes squeaking on the linoleum floor as he shifted direction. Outside the window the rain, the psychiatrist became aware, had stopped. The sky was very black, starless.

"Further tests will have to be made, but it is possible that there is something wrong with your brain that could be cured by surgery. I will speak to the people in charge here."

The patient stood still and said, "They will never let me leave, particularly not if there has been some mistake."

"It won't be right away, and it will be tricky, but I promise you I will see you get the necessary tests." The psychiatrist looked at his watch. He added, "I'm afraid it is very late now. I have to catch the last train in half an hour." He stood up and put on his coat and gloves.

The patient moved with such sudden speed and in such an unforeseen manner that the psychiatrist was unable to react. He had his hands on the collar of the psychiatrist's coat. He said, "I'm certain we have met somewhere before."

The psychiatrist wanted to tell him that patients often told him that; that he had patients waiting for him in the city; that if he missed his train he would have to spend the night up here in a stranger's house; and that he hated the country. But he looked into the man's face and saw the hope in his eyes.

The psychiatrist thought of his own mother, a tall redhead with a commanding nose, a considerable bosom and a Midwestern drawl, who had promised every year to take him to Europe and, instead, gave the money she had saved for the trip to charity. Then he sat down again and took off his leather gloves.

The elderly doctor drove them back to his house. It was surrounded by slender white birch, and all the lights were lit. When they walked into the hall, the psychiatrist could smell something cooking. Though he had eaten almost nothing all day, the strong odor made him feel slightly sick. He was ushered into a stuffy, cluttered living room and was left alone. He walked uncomfortably across the thick carpet, looking at the pathetic signs of cheap luxury, strewn around the room: the gilt candelabra, the brocade slipcovers, the tasseled poufs. It was very warm in the room, and through the thin walls the psychiatrist could hear much anxious muttering and the clattering of dishes. He heard something fall to the floor and a little shriek followed by what sounded like a slap. Suddenly a strange, thin sound struck up: a monotonous, whining voice, singing a sad song. The music rose and fell endlessly and evoked strange, unpleasant echoes in the psychiatrist's mind. He was certain he had heard it before. For a moment he felt slightly giddy, and then his heart started to beat irregularly, once again. He collapsed on the sofa, bent over. He put his hand over his mouth.

When he looked up, he realized he was being watched. A slim young woman in a bright pink dress, which looked too big for her, was standing shyly by the door. She wore gold sandals with high heels and her long black hair loose. It glowed, glossy as a blackbird. There was, incongruously, a lily, whose odor perfumed the air, pinned in her locks. She smiled and then walked toward him, swinging her hips gracefully, holding her small head high, a tray poised in one hand. She placed the tray carefully on the table.

Since his wife's departure, the psychiatrist had avoided painful entanglements with women, but he would have liked to seduce them, all of them, indiscriminately. As he walked down a street, he took them with his eyes, the thin and the fat, the young and the old, the pretty and the ugly. This one looked at him with her steady, dark gaze.

The psychiatrist stood up, introduced himself, and reached out to shake the girl's small, warm hand. It seemed to him she held onto his hand for a moment longer than necessary. He felt the soft skin lingering against his own. The girl introduced herself solemnly as the elderly doctor's youngest daughter. "So pleased to meet you," she said in a high voice. She disengaged her hand to pour something carefully from the pitcher on the tray into a small glass and handed it to him with a napkin. All the while he was sipping the sweet liqueur and wiping his mouth, she watched him intently. It seemed to the psychiatrist that the girl had the same hopeful stare in her eyes as had the patient in the institution.

The dinner table was arrayed with a vast number of dishes in heavy sauces, though only two places were laid. There were flowers floating in a gilt bowl of water in the center, and the yellow candles were lit. The elderly doctor and the young psychiatrist dined alone, sitting opposite one another at one end of the table.

The psychiatrist asked if the doctor's wife would not join them and thought of his own ex-wife, a woman with the unusual combination of dark hair and bright blue eyes, whose idea of dinner was a jar of peanut butter left on the table with a knife in it. She had told him before leaving that she found him boring and critical, had run up his credit card bills, and then run off with a rock star.

The elderly doctor looked down at the table and said his wife had not recovered completely after an illness. She was troubled by shingles brought on, most likely, by stress.

The psychiatrist asked how many children the elderly doctor had. He smiled and said God had been good to him; he had six, and many grandchildren as well, though, of course, the burden of providing for such a large family fell on his shoulders most heavily at times, and he looked at the psychiatrist and added that he was sure he would understand.

The psychiatrist said that, indeed, he did, that he himself had two small boys, and that that was quite heavy enough for him. Then the elderly doctor clicked his fingers, and the daughter who had served the drinks came in with a plate of warm, buttered bread, covered with a linen napkin. She served the psychiatrist with the same hopeful gaze, lingering close beside him, so that he could smell the strong odor of lilies.

He said he was sorry not to make the wife's acquaintance, and turned toward the girl and added that the elderly doctor had a very lovely daughter, indeed. The doctor smiled and gestured to the girl to come closer to him. He reached up and spread his fingers gently and proprietorially over her bare shoulder and said that to him all his daughters were lovely. She leaned down against him, her dark, glossy head touching his, smiling as if for a photograph. The psychiatrist thought with longing of his two dark-haired and blue-eyed boys, whom he could now see only every other weekend. The doctor's daughter left the room, swinging her slender hips gracefully, but it seemed to the psychiatrist that her odor lingered.

The elderly doctor drank several glasses of wine and urged the psychiatrist to drink and eat. He said that wine gave him a headache and that he was not very hungry. The bread was heavy and tasteless, and the dishes so heavily spiced, they brought tears to his eyes. He asked for an aspirin and explained that he had trouble with his heart from time to time—arrhythmia, he said. The elderly doctor clicked his tongue and told him to watch out for stroke.

The singing in the background was softer now but continued monotonously. The room grew hotter, the lily scent heavier. The psychiatrist loosened his tie, asked if the elderly doctor would mind if he removed his jacket. He was sweating and feeling increasingly unwell. At first he could not concentrate at all on what the elderly doctor was saying, waiting only for the moment to broach the subject of the patient, but after a while, he found himself listening as the doctor went on rapidly and at length about the institution.

There was something almost incantatory about the elderly doctor's accented words with their singsong cadence, their old-fashioned formality. He said that on the whole he could say without lying that the patients were really quite contented in that place. Of course, one could not hope to cure them—how could one hope to cure such people? God's will would be done, what was bound to be could not be otherwise—but in his humble opinion many of the patients seemed much improved. They even put on plays themselves from time to time; the eminent psychiatrist should really try to find time in his busy schedule to attend. The spectacle was really most edifying, and there were many diverse workshops to keep the patients busy: basket weaving, music therapy, art therapy. There was even a rather large indoor swimming pool for them. The swimming seemed, in his modest opinion, to be most helpful, the elderly doctor said. Occasionally some of the patients were even given the opportunity to go horseback riding on a nearby farm. If only the eminent psychiatrist could see their glowing faces when they came back from a ride! What a gratifying sight! Truly, many of them had grown very much attached to the people in charge who, though they did not always have the highest qualifications—unfortunately it was not always possible to get people with the highest qualifications to come up to a place like this and to work with patients of this sort—were very sensitive to the patients' needs. Everyone, the elderly doctor said, as he looked at the psychiatrist anxiously, was doing his very best.

The psychiatrist interrupted and said he was certain they were doing their best. Then he attempted to speak of the patient he had seen that afternoon, but his head was spinning and his heartbeat irregular, and he had felt obliged to drink some of the sweet wine, which made him feel even worse. It seemed to him that the cloying, strong scent of lilies added to his nausea.

He suggested that certain tests should be made, to determine whether the origin of the patient's behavior might be organic.

"Organic!" the elderly doctor exclaimed and clasped his fine hands together dramatically. The psychiatrist asked if there was any good reason why routine tests of this sort had never been done. The doctor said he was sure such tests were not necessary, and that in his opinion if such a thing were discovered, which seemed extremely doubtful—after all, the diagnosis of mental illness had been made several years earlier, just before the doctor had arrived there—the patient would in any event be unwilling, if one could speak of his having a will at all, to go through anything as traumatic as surgery, but naturally he, as the doctor-in-charge of the mental institution, would follow the eminent psychiatrist's suggestion. With a trembling hand he passed a dish of stewed chicken which lay swimming in its oily sauce.

The psychiatrist declined, said he was feeling very tired. The elderly doctor went on talking about the hospital, giving the psychiatrist all sorts of details and using many learned terms.

The room the psychiatrist was to occupy for the night was small and airless. He did not undress fully but lay in his shirt and socks, tossing back and forth. His head continued to ache, and he felt unwell. The odor of lilies lingered in the hot air. His heart beat irregularly. He heard strange rustlings and murmuring from the room next door. He could see a light under the door. He had the impression he was being watched. Finally, toward morning, he put his coat back on, staggered down the stairs, and went outside into the cool air.

A faint beam of light pierced the clouds, and the psychiatrist could make out the mental institution in the distance; it glimmered white as a ghost in the early mist. He thought of the man shut up in there, year after year, his movements constantly watched, his breathing stifled by the mask. He heard the patient's words: "All I want is to leave this place."

As he looked up into the branches of a slim birch tree in the muted light of day, a memory came to him. Standing in the faint first light, his heart beating irregularly, the sweat trickling down his forehead, his vision dim, he seemed to see his own father's tall figure, caught in a beam of light from the open door, standing darkly in the hall. It was the day his father left their house for the war, never to come back. The psychiatrist saw his mother's face as she bent over him, watching him with that anxious light in her dark eyes. He smelled the panic on her breath, as she drew her face closer and closer to his and held him ever more tightly in her arms, until his ribs ached. She was whispering words to him, words he was never to forget. She was saying that he would have to take care of her now, that he would have to be her *good, good* boy, that he would have to be her *little man.*

In that instant the psychiatrist realized what it had all been leading toward—the spotlessness of his clothes, the orderliness of his room, the smoothness of his bed, the boat he had carved in wood, the hands kept outside the blanket all through the long night, the piles of clean dishes, the cleaned oven, the shoveled snow, the repaired lamps, the endless studies, the excellent grades, the carefully reasoned prescriptions, the brilliant interpretations, the published articles, the endless hours of listening and listening. He thought of the art studies he had abandoned, and the long hours he had spent in museums looking at paintings he had loved. He remembered one fall afternoon in Paris on his junior year abroad when he had sat outside in a cafe near the Seine and felt the sun on his shoulders and sipped a delicious, strong, dark espresso with a little sliver of lemon peel. He thought of the plane ride he had taken to London and how he had arrived there unexpectedly to propose to his ex-wife. He remembered a line from a poem that he had never really understood: "Else a great prince in a prison lies." In one instant he realized where it had all taken him, what it all meant.

As he was thinking this, he heard the same sound he had heard the night before, the same strange, whining sound, the sad voice singing its ancient and incomprehensible song. It shattered the silence of the early morning. It seemed to him that it was this music that made him feel so unwell.

He hurried back inside and picked up his watch from beside the bed. He walked down the corridor and knocked loudly on the bedroom door. The elderly doctor emerged almost immediately and fully dressed, as though he had been waiting for the psychiatrist's knock. He asked the doctor to drive him to the station in order to catch the early morning train. The elderly doctor did not offer him breakfast but told him to wait in the hall.

The psychiatrist could hear the sound of the car's wheels spinning on the stones of the driveway. The doctor drove the car to the front door and jumped out with alacrity to usher the psychiatrist into the front seat. He drove the psychiatrist fast and in silence to the station, as though he were afraid the psychiatrist might change his mind on the way. The elderly doctor shook the psychiatrist's hand warmly as he thanked him for his hospitality, and almost pushed the psychiatrist up the steps to the platform.

The elderly doctor stood grinning and waving enthusiastically as the train drew out of the station.

Death in Rome

T he room, indeed, looks tomb-like, she thinks, but,
naturally, does not say. There are no windows, only sky-
lights in the roof, covered by blinds raised electrically. The
bellhop shows them how—pushing a button that makes a
mournful whirring sound. Pale, striped silk covers the walls,
and a sad blue carpet, the floor. The ceiling slopes so that she
cannot stand to her full height in parts of the room.

A tall, angular woman, Ada does not like small, cramped
spaces; they make her breathless. She feels even taller beside
her small Italian friend. Laura had warned her on the phone it
might be difficult to find a room in Rome because of the
coming jubilee. "I must have called a hundred places—there
was just nothing else," Laura apologizes in her soft liquescent
language, blinking gray short-sighted eyes.

"Absolutely fine," Ada replies in rusty Italian, and hunts for
money in her voluminous black bag. She can never find
anything in the confusion of notes for her work. Her gaze falls
on one, "One way is to invent a kind of neutralizing middle

voice that is neither abstractly and impersonally cold nor directly emotional and dramatic, but one that lies in that gray limbo." When had she written that and why?

Laura gives the bellhop a tip and thanks him with a smile that shows small, almost good teeth. He smiles back and says something Ada does not understand as he shuts the door quietly behind him. Ada hears the click and thinks of her West Side apartment in New York with its large, half-empty white rooms, high ceilings, bookcases and long windows. She surveys the two narrow beds set side by side with their shiny pink counterpanes and contemplates sharing a room with someone as though she were a child again. But she says, "Bathroom's great," as cheerfully as possible, peering warily into the dimness of the windowless room.

Ada was brought up to struggle valiantly against adversity—"Where there's a will, there's a way," her Scottish nanny would say—but she wonders if she has mistaken her way. She had saved up her frequent flyer miles, and she so wanted to see Laura, to give her a few luxurious days in Rome before it was too late. Also, she had been seized by a sudden and strange impulse to travel—to leave everything behind, and above all the constant tension of her career.

But what has she done? She wants to run out of the place as she squints at the narrow, coffin-like tub, the useless bidet, and the ironed linen hand towels that look as though they belong in a church and which neither of them will dare use.

"Besides, we'll be out most of the time. Let's hurry and unpack and go out. I can't wait to see the new rooms at the Borghese!" Ada exclaims and piles up all the heavy tomes she has brought to read, throws her underwear and sweaters into the drawers. Laura balances her toilet bag on the edge of the basin and hangs up the blue linen dress Ada gave her years ago which still looks as good as new.

"We must see if we can get tickets for a concert, perhaps. And I want to rent a car and drive out to Tivoli one day," Ada proposes.

Laura murmurs gently, "Tivoli might be a bit crowded," and sits down on the end of the bed for a moment, breathing heavily. Ada thinks Laura's color is not good: dead white against the dark of her short, soft curls.

What will she do if Laura is taken seriously ill here? How would she manage if Laura were to die in this city where organized chaos reigns? How could she manage anywhere? She wonders if this will be the last time they are together.

Laura has visited Ada every year, arriving like summer, dropping small hand-made presents for Ada's children, as she gathered them up in her arms. Ada's two thin serious girls would leave their books and their beds to roam the countryside with her, hunting mushrooms, learning to bake, singing Italian songs: *Gira gira tondo, Casca il mondo, Tutti giu per terra*, all holding hands and throwing themselves on the ground with abandon. Ada's husband, also from Bologna, behaved as though Laura had cast a spell on him—rushing home early for dinner with the children, sitting with Laura and the girls on the nursery floor, setting up the doll's house; learning to make spaghetti Bolognese according to Laura's mother's recipe—cutting up onions and simmering red wine and stirring in freshly chopped tomatoes, and he, who was never interested in Ada's work, talking for hours about Pavese, Silone, Svevo and the Italian novel.

Together, Ada and Laura, with the two little girls in tow, voyaged, Laura leading the way, guide book in hand, going through all the Roman arenas in Provence, the castles of the Loire valley, the Romanesque churches of Tuscany.

Now Laura's twilight gray gaze glimmers behind her contact lenses and meets Ada's with misty affection. She reaches out and grasps Ada's hand. "It's such a treat to see you, dear. I'm so grateful you made the long tiring trip for me," Laura says softly, holding onto Ada with her hot little hand.

"Do you want to rest for a bit, darling?" Ada inquires, disengaging, turning her gaze away.

"No, no, just catching my breath," Laura reassures her and smiles.

"I could go out on my own, perhaps?" Ada suggests. She wouldn't mind walking around for a while on her own. She might look into that good bookstore she discovered off Via del Corso and see which new books have been translated into Italian. Perhaps there might even be some of her work.

The street, Via del Corso, seems endless. In the great swarm of people, they can hardly walk along the narrow pavement. The noise of cars and the buzzing of the motor scooters obliges them to shout. Exhaust fumes assail them. It is a splendid Roman October, the light gold, the sky pale blue, the air warm, almost summer-like. Ada sweats in her black pantsuit and black blouse. She should have worn something lighter like the simple blue linen dress Laura is wearing. Saddest of all, beautiful Rome lies buried under multiple layers of gauze in preparation for the Jubilee. Everything is muffled and masked under scaffolding, as though for surgery.

Laura takes Ada's arm, leans a little, and from time to time in the crush, her full firm breast brushes against Ada. Laura, who has never married or had children, has kept her figure and her youthful curves. The proximity of her plump, soft body makes Ada uncomfortable, but she thinks Laura is not aware of the possibilities of such closeness. Laura seems to have preserved a sort of innocence over all these years.

"Can you make it to the Borghese, or shall we hail a taxi?" Ada asks her friend.

"No, no, there's no need," Laura says. Ada walks behind her and places her hand on her back to help her up the steep hill.

But in the museum Ada listens to Laura's gasping and accosts a guard. "Angelo's the one with the keys," he says. Angelo is tall and fresh-cheeked with blond dreadlocks and a gold ring in his ear—impossibly handsome as perhaps only Roman men can be. He looks at them and says the elevator is reserved for the old and those who cannot climb stairs. "My friend *needs* the elevator," Ada insists.

"I have been very ill," Laura whispers, her delicate hand to her chest. She lowers her twilight-gray gaze with the modesty that overtakes her when she speaks of her illness. She looks like a bride speaking with modest pride of her coming wedding, or a young mother hinting with embarrassment and awe at the new life she carries within her.

Indeed, Ada thinks, Laura's skin is still smooth and has the translucency that comes from living life innocently. Laura has lived with her mother and taught school to small children in the mornings. Ada imagines Laura has prayed away any desire or aggression she might have felt in long hours on her knees in the shadows of Gothic churches. Ada, who has married and divorced and struggled to attain success in a long and difficult career, knows she has many lines around her faded blue eyes, her thin mouth. She has small brown age spots on her forehead and hands. But Laura's ribs have been cracked to remove her cancered lung; she has lain through the summer in the heat of a crowded public hospital sucking desperately for air through a tube which did not always function. She has followed several chemotherapy treatments that left her hairless, prostrate, and slowly suffocating. Now Laura's lovely dark hair has grown back, and she has less difficulty breathing, but still cannot climb stairs.

"Well, if you wish," Angelo says, smiling at Laura and taking out the keys. He asks Laura if he has not met her somewhere before, but she smiles and shakes her head and says people often ask her that, she must have that sort of face. In the small space of the dark, paneled elevator, Ada removes her jacket, tugs at the high neck of her blouse, breathless herself, stains of sweat appearing under the armpits of her blouse. They ascend slowly. "Very old," Ada says nervously, lifting her gaze toward the painted ceiling.

"Only about fifty years," Angelo demurs as though he has lived forever. He smiles with the clear blue eyes and the rosy lips his name indicates. The irony of this passes in silence. He refuses Ada's tip. Perhaps she had not given him enough, Ada thinks, as they step forth into, indeed, paradise.

The master works are here: the Caravaggios, the Raphaels, the Peruginos. Ada, who has an advanced degree in psychology, drags Laura by the arm over to the Leda in one of the rooms. "Da Vinci," she exclaims and gives Freud's explanation for the loveliness of the woman's face. "He was thinking of his mother's face. She had given him up to another woman with better prospects, but he always remembered her."

"A copy," Laura says lightly and leads her to a corner of the room.

Before Perugino's little Madonna and child Laura whispers as if she were in a holy place, "Raphael's master." She coughs a little. "See the pale blue sky—Raphael learned that from him." She goes on to explain the inscription above another painting—"the muses" she explains, "Clio was the muse of history," she begins and recites the names of all the rest.

Ada thinks sadly that Laura, who has often hidden her knowledge out of modesty, is now willing to share it, as though she wishes to take this last opportunity to tell her friend everything she knows. Or perhaps the presence of death makes her believe there is no longer any need for deception.

"Notice the slight difference between the color of the dead Christ's flesh and that of the others," Laura points out, leading Ada to Raphael's, "Descent from the Cross."

"Yes, you are right," Ada replies stiffly. She attempts to avoid the subject of death at any cost—even the word, if it comes up, and it seems to keep coming up. She walks on quickly to Raphael's pink-cheeked blond-haired girl. Ada says, "Look at the little lamb in her arm."

"A unicorn, isn't it? See the horn," Laura indicates.

Ada suggests they sit down on the Via Veneto. She sits in the shade and puts Laura where she prefers, in the sun. "Heavenly," Laura says, scooping up the cream and sugar from the bottom of her cup. "Why is it only Italians can make coffee that tastes this good?" Ada asks Laura, but Laura has her eyes shut, her head tilted back. She has opened her small mouth slightly. The sun is on the smooth oval of her face like warm water. Perhaps everything will all be all right. Perhaps Laura will live forever.

Ada hears a loud noise. A man strums a guitar, bending forward from the waist and smiling unctuously, singing off key right in her ear. He tries to make up for his lack of voice with much absurd mimicry of the opera singer's art. He waves his arms around, opens his mouth, struts back and forth, beats his chest.

"Oh, God," Ada exclaims, raises her eyebrows and hunts for a coin in the depths of her black bag. But the man goes on strumming, bending nearer to her, gesticulating and laughing ingratiatingly. His antics distort his features into a grimacing mask with a rictus-like smile. He makes the rounds of the tables, cap outstretched, bowing and saying in a self-mocking tone, "Pavarotti," and then doubling over with laughter.

Ada finds herself saying, "He makes me think of the scene in that work by Mann. Is it *Mario and the Magician*?"

Laura looks at her and murmurs, "No, no, it's not Mario, of course, it's Aschenbach, it's *Death in Venice*—"and they look at one another in silence. Every reference to death is like an obscene remark, Ada thinks.

Now Ada says *she* is really exhausted and famished. She feels the jet lag, all her work to finish her new novel prior to her trip. They must find a place nearby for lunch. Laura lifts her map to her short-sighted eyes and indicates a shady restaurant in a quiet square. Despite poor eyesight, she seems able to find her way in any city.

Laura contemplates the menu avidly and says she would like the spaghetti carbonara. Ada attempts a joke about her high cholesterol—which she inherited from her father, who died young, but it catches in her throat.

"So when do you go for your award?" Laura asks when her spaghetti arrives, watching Ada eat her salad with no dressing.

Ada tries not to talk about her work with Laura—it seems in bad taste, at a time like this, but that, too, like death, slips out every now and then.

"I go next week. Imagine, an award from such an illustrious man!" she cannot resist exclaiming. The judge is a world-renowned writer.

"You have done so remarkably well," Laura smiles with real admiration in her large gray eyes and squeezes Ada's hand.

"Lots of hard work," Ada murmurs with an attempt at modesty.

It is true that Ada has worked hard. Since her divorce and the children's leaving home, her life has gradually been consumed by work. Now she can hardly even imagine any pleasure not associated with work. She lives alone and works all the time—rising at dawn, running around the reservoir, showering and sitting down at her desk before nine, answering letters, arranging readings, lectures, before attacking her writing. She works on trains, buses, airplanes, even during jury duty. Every moment of her day and much of her night is given over to the difficult discipline of her work. She does her best work in the dead of night rising and going to her desk and working with a sort of dream-like intensity. She wonders what Laura might have done with her excellent mind if she had been more ambitious.

"And what will you wear? You must have your lovely hair done for the award giving. Wear it down. I like it down," Laura says smiling affectionately and with no hint of jealousy, and reaching across the table to touch a strand of Ada's blond hair which she wears punished with pins into a bun at the nape of her neck. Ada pulls back, shakes her head and shrugs and says she does not care about her appearance; what she is worrying about is what she will say to the eminent writer and who will attend the ceremony.

After lunch, Ada insists that Laura remain in the room and rest. She gives Laura a story she has just written and leaves her lying on the bed struggling with the difficult English sentences, while Ada rushes off down Via del Corso in the heat of the day. She makes her way rapidly through the crowd and dashes into the bookstore she remembers. She climbs the stairs two at a time, and hurriedly hunts through the rows of books, her heart thumping as she scans the volumes to see if the Italian translation of her latest book is there. She asks the salesman for the book, not mentioning that it is hers. He looks it up on his computer and offers to order it.

"I will only be here a few days," she says.

He promises to get the book for her by then and charges her in advance. Ada pays the considerable sum, hoping that the man will not notice her photograph on the back of the book. She will pick it up on the day she leaves.

"Where did you go?" Laura asks, when Ada rushes, sweating and breathless, back into the room.

"Just wandered around a bit," Ada lies. "What did you think of the story?" she asks eagerly.

"The English was too hard for me, I'm afraid. You look awfully hot," Laura says, smiling at her.

At dinner, Ada orders steak for both of them and a bottle of expensive red wine. "It's delicious," Laura says, sipping from her glass.

"I just want you to have a lovely, lovely time," Ada replies and watches her eating and drinking with obvious pleasure.

How Italians take pleasure from the small things of life, she thinks.

Ada grins at Laura and says, "Do you remember the lasagna?"

Laura laughs and groans, "That dreadful, dreadful car ride."

They were both nineteen—Laura, a young inexperienced student and Ada, a young inexperienced mother, newly arrived with her baby and young husband in Italy to visit her in-laws. They had picked Laura up in Ada's husband's fancy new car and then driven fast down the ancient winding road toward the sea, going to her mother-in-law's villa where they had left their baby girl. Laura, whose own mother—convinced she would starve with these foreigners—had fed her a huge farewell dinner of lasagna, was violently sick all over the new red leather of the car. Horribly embarrassed, Laura kept saying, *"Che vergogna, che vergogna."*

"And then you went off and left me all alone in the villa for three days," Laura says in a matter-of-fact voice, staring at her well-manicured nails.

"It's not possible. I remember only one evening. I remember showing you how to make the bottle for the baby and then going off to the opera in Verona, and surely Nonna was there," Ada protests.

"No, no, it was three days. And your mother-in-law disappeared that night, too—she went off to see her sister, I think, and your father-in-law escaped to spend the night at his club. I had to call my mother to ask her how to care for the baby."

Ada says, "How could they have done that?"

Laura says, "You didn't even show me poor little Sally, because she was asleep. And your father-in-law left five thousand lire on the floor to find out if I was honest. But I could have stolen the baby or drowned her in the bath!!"

"Oh God, how awful," Ada says but wonders why Laura has to mention it at this point. Why does Laura want to make her feel guilty? "I'm sure it was only one evening that we were away," Ada insists and gives her friend a reproachful look.

"No, no, I assure you. And when you came back you left the baby with me and your mother-in-law in the villa, and you and Sergio stayed on your own at the Royal."

"We did that?" Ada says, appalled. Surely she would never have done such a thing!

"You seemed like a different person, then," Laura says, looking at Ada with wonderment.

Ada reflects. She can imagine Sergio convincing her to leave the baby with his mother and the baby sitter and stay with him at a hotel on their own, convincing her, convincing anyone for that matter, of anything in those days. She sees him now as she saw him for the first time striding through the gate and into the Grand Hotel garden where she was having tea with her mother—a tall, blond young Bolognese in white linen pants, his shirt sleeves turned up to the elbows, with the wide charming smile of the pampered Italian boy, the smile that said—"Of course you will do what I want! Everyone always has. How could you not?" And indeed they did. He remains the most charming man she has ever met, she thinks.

She says, "Oh God, Laura, you know you're probably right. We were so young and so dumb."

Now it all comes back to her—that summer on the Italian Riviera when they first met Laura, the brilliance of the light, the soft murmur of the shimmering sea, the sound of the wind in the pines; how she and Sergio had played tennis at the club in the afternoons, their long legs tanned in white shorts. People often took them for brother and sister in those days: both blond and tall and full of energy—how they had struck out, swimming for miles in the calm sea, and then thrown themselves down in the sun on the hot sand; how they had drunk white wine and eaten oysters on the terrace under a sky with a wandering moon followed by stars; how they had made love in the warm nights, rolling around on the big soft bed and laughing at the least little thing—how crazy in love they had been. They had reached out to life and grasped it, without considering the consequences. Then it had all come crashing down. She had begun to rise in the nights to work, to refuse to take naps in the afternoons, to walk about thinking of her characters and not Sergio. There were quarrels, recriminations, remorse. How far away all of that now seems.

She asks Laura, "Is there anything *you* regret doing?"

There is a moment of silence at the table. Laura lifts her glass of wine and looks across the table at Ada as though there were something she would like to say. But she shakes her head and then says, "You know miracles have happened to me since I fell ill."

"Miracles?"

"There was my mother, for example, after all those years of making my life miserable, deciding suddenly that she would go to a home and leave the apartment all to me, so that for the first time I can invite whomever I wish to stay."

Ada says, "She must have realized you couldn't take care of her anymore," and thinks of the irony of Laura who loves everyone, and whom everyone loves, living out her life with someone she should have loved the most but never could.

She says, "Laura, darling, I want you to know that I am here for you if you need me. I don't want you to have to suffer through this alone." But she believes Laura will not ask her to come to her, though she would go if she were asked. Laura will not ask anyone to come to her—except her priest. She will do her suffering alone, or anyway alone with her God.

Laura leans forward and reaches out for Ada's hand. Ada feels the grip of the hot fingers and shivers slightly as Laura says in a low voice, her eyes shining, "I believe our suffering has a meaning. Jesus suffered to give us eternal life. I believe we *will* see one another again. We will exist eternally," squeezing Ada's hand, her face glowing with conviction.

Tears blind Ada, and she wants to tell her friend that ever since she heard of her illness she has gone to church each Sunday to pray to a God in whom she is not sure she believes. Sometimes Ada thinks it is her prayers that have kept Laura alive. Sometimes she also imagines Laura's prayers—for she is certain Laura prays for her—have helped her with her own life. She realizes that Laura is trying to comfort *her*, to make this easy for her, as though she were the one in need of comfort, as though it were she who were doing the dying. She says softly, "I do so hope you are right," and puts her hand to her chest where she feels a heavy weight.

That night, Laura lies at length in the bath—she loves hot baths, Ada knows, scented water, oils. Ada sits at the desk and struggles to comprehend the heavy tome by the eminent writer who has selected her for the award. Laura emerges from the bathroom in a short pink gown, smelling sweet, her skin dewy. Exhausted by the long day, Ada shyly dons her long white nightdress in the bathroom and jumps quickly into bed. But Laura is already lying on her back, her breath quiet, her eyes closed, her dark curls on the pillow. Ada turns out the light but cannot sleep. What will she say to the brilliant writer? Much of his heavy tome is obscure, unnecessarily long-winded in her opinion, though there are flashes of brilliance she envies. She thinks of the people she must remember to call on her return to make sure there will be a good crowd at the event. What if no one comes? And what will the critics say about her new work? She remembers a harsh review in which her last work had been called a *tour de force*, distanced from the reader, elegant sentences without any real emotion.

Her eyes puffy from lack of sleep, Ada, followed by Laura, staggers into the underground breakfast room. A buffet spreads out on the long table before them: cold meats, cheeses, different cereals, breads, sticky buns, and croissants. There is a silver urn with hot coffee and big jugs of frothy hot milk. Laura exclaims, "Look how lovely!" and claps her hands. She heaps up her plate with croissants and slips a few packages of *Bel Paese*, in round silver paper packages with the map of Italy on the front, into her pockets. Ada takes a croissant and a small cup of black coffee. Laura, who is not adverse to a bargain, says, "Eat up, Ada. Let's tuck in, then we won't need lunch."

"This is plenty for me," Ada replies. She is not hungry.

When they emerge, blinking into the sunlight, Laura offers to drive the rented car. "Are you sure?" Ada asks.

"Yes, yes, I feel much better today."

"You are certainly better at finding your way than I am," Ada assents, happy to take what is known as the "death seat." She opens the window to let the breeze blow on her, leans back, feels the gold light on her face. She is suddenly content to be sitting down after all the walking, the churches, her sleepless night. She intends to doze, but Laura drives surprisingly fast, aggressively, winding back and forth, honking her horn. She complains constantly about the other drivers, the rudeness of the Romans—*Prepotenti*, she shouts, slamming on the brakes, drumming her little fist on the wheel. To her surprise Ada even hears Laura say something about a *Porco-cane*, a pig dog, and even a *stronzo*, which Ada thinks might actually have something to do with shit. Ada smiles, but reflects she should have driven, herself. She has forgotten how Laura becomes a different person behind the wheel. Ada keeps slamming her foot on an imaginary brake and sucking in the air through her teeth, as Laura passes dangerously on the narrow curving country road. Ada feels nauseated. She should have eaten more breakfast. Lately, she has been losing weight. Sometimes she is so absorbed by her work she forgets to eat, to drink, even to rise to go to the bathroom. Laura suggests they avoid the crowds at Tivoli and go to Hadrian's villa instead. "Besides, it's nearer. You look a little green," Laura says glancing at her friend and shifting gears fast.

"Wherever you want to go," Ada murmurs, too ill to argue, the bile rising ominously in her mouth.

At Hadrian's villa, Laura halts the car abruptly in the parking lot. She springs out, leads the way across wide green fields strewn with small blue flowers. "Come on Ad," she calls. Ada sits stunned in the sudden quiet and then drags herself out. Ada is surprised by the deep shadows of the pine trees, the wide spaces. The silence is different from anything she has ever experienced, broken only by something that sounds almost like a whirring of wings—an airplane, perhaps. "You are my cicerone," Ada says weakly, laying her hand on Laura's shoulder, leaning on her, going down the stone steps to where the vast pool lies with the caryatids at its side.

"Thanks to you I feel so much better," Laura says, looking back over her shoulder. Indeed, she seems to have found new energy, vigor. Ada notices the strong, smooth muscles of her calves. Laura, who has always been an excellent walker, who has led her and the children over the mountain paths, now goes fast ahead.

"Let's sit down," Ada suggests. They sit on a bench in the shade, and Laura tells Ada about the different emperors: Nero, who had his stepfather killed and his stepbrother, Brittanicus, and then killed his own mother, too. Laura, who knows Latin, translates the inscriptions on the old stones.

"How much you know!" Ada says, looking at her wonderingly and with some embarrassment, remembering the year Laura spent with them in New York and how hard she had worked with the children, and how she would dash off for an hour or two to go to the library, she said, to read for her thesis on the influence of the American writers on Pavese.

Then Laura says, "You know, I had a lovely letter from Sergio recently." She tilts her delicate head toward the sun like an oval bud on the long stem of her neck, the petals of the gold scarf she wears around her shoulders making her skin glow. Her face looks younger than ever and, Ada thinks, somehow naked. Ada stares at her and would like to ask what she does to her skin to make it glow.

She says, "Really? I haven't heard from him for ages," surprised to feel a little pang of jealousy after all these years. But she adds quickly, "I'm so glad he thought to write to you. I must have mentioned you had been ill in a letter. For all his faults, I have to say he is a sentimental man, and I know he was always very fond of you," remembering him drinking a whole bottle of whiskey and weeping the night he had told her he had fallen in love with another woman.

"I asked him to come and see me—it's been so hard recently on my own, you understand, and now that Mother is gone, I can ask whomever I want. I thought you should know, he did come," Laura says, smiling softly and putting her hot hand gently on Ada's knee. She turns to Laura and gazes into her twilight gray eyes. She has never noticed before what fine eyes Laura has, the lashes dark and heavy. Ada feels a little shiver of something she has not felt for many years, that she can only call desire.

"You did? He did?" Ada says.

"I thought under the circumstances, you wouldn't mind," Laura murmurs.

"Of course not! Why would I mind?" Ada asks, but she feels suddenly as if her heart has stopped. She sits quite still waiting for it to start up again, watching the glint of light on the dark water.

"Caro Sergio—just as extravagant as ever. He insisted on us staying at the Royal," Laura laughs. Ada cannot reply. She cannot move, a sort of languor spreading through her veins like wine.

"You are such a forgiving person, Ada—the most forgiving person I know, a true Christian," Laura says and shakes her head with wonderment and strokes Ada's bare knee softly.

The autumnal light is pale on the vast dome of the Pantheon. The breeze blows the water against Ada's face. Tourists throng the square near their hotel, and a gypsy woman in a long tattered gown swings up to them, begging for money in exchange for good luck. Ada waves her away impatiently.

She feels a sudden dizziness.

She had promised to take Laura to the train station herself and put her on her train and leave from there to the airport, but she has decided to say good-bye to Laura at the taxi station in the square, to pick up her book from the bookstore, and then take a taxi directly to the airport and not bother with the train. Ada has said she does not like lengthy good-byes. She has paid the hotel bill, bought Laura a new silk scarf, and helped Laura down the stairs with her baggage.

"No, no, I will do it," Ada insists, carrying Laura's baggage to the taxi. It is surprisingly heavy. As she puts it down on the ground for a moment, flexes her fingers, Laura says, "I didn't want to say anything that might hurt, Ada, but I felt you should know the truth, after all these years. In the end it does not help to go through life blind."

Ada catches her breath but says nothing. What can she say? As she lifts the suitcase to hand it to the taxi-driver, she feels a stab of pain in her chest. Laura puts her arms around her friend and holds her close. Ada can feel the warmth and comfort of her plump, firm body.

Laura says stiffly, disengaging herself, "I don't know how to thank you for taking the time from your busy schedule to come all this way and spend these days with me. Your presence has restored me."

Ada looks at her and says, "Indeed, Laura, you do look restored." Her skin glows and her hair, catching the sunlight, is full of red lights. Ada swallows and says, "But there is no reason to thank me. It has been my great pleasure—a good excuse to spend a few days in Rome, to get away from everything." Laura steps into the taxi and peers shortsightedly through the back window. She is smiling at Ada radiantly and with sympathy, and she is moving her small hand. She seems to Ada to be summoning her, to be beckoning. For a moment Ada wants to call out, "Don't leave me here alone! I'll lose my way," but instead she stands and waves, following the black taxi with her gaze.

It is the last time Ada sees Laura.

She glances at her watch. She will just have time to rush to the shop to pick up her book. But she feels suddenly tired—all the walking and sightseeing has worn her out unduly, surely, and there is that heavy weight pressing down on her chest. Ada climbs the stairs to her windowless hotel room to lie down for just a moment on the bed before she picks up her precious purchase. She imagines herself standing on the platform and receiving her award from the eminent writer to great applause. She closes the shutters, pressing the button and listening to the whirring sound.

Rain Check

My husband has taken a mistress, so I take out my address book and run my finger down the names of the men I used to know. I write to several, and one writes back from Africa. He takes people out hunting—what used to be called a Great White Hunter. I remember lying beside him on the sand, my head propped on a deadwood branch under the fever trees. The Great White Hunter is trying to unbutton my blouse, but I am watching the dark, swift-moving waters of the wide river and the sudden flash of brilliance as a king-fisher dives for its prey.

Now his agency is sending him to Paris to hunt for new clients.

I walk through the empty rooms that look onto formal French gardens and stand at the open window, waiting for him. Policemen in blue capes are closing the iron gates and blowing their whistles. A child cries, dragged reluctantly down a dusty path. A fan-shaped sprinkler catches the evening light in the spray.

He still has the sun-bleached yellow hair and the broad shoulders. For a moment when he enters, in my panic, I cannot remember his name. When he holds me to kiss me on the cheek, his eyes seem so close set and such a deep blue, looking into them is like looking into a double-barreled gun. I say, "Michael! How amazing!" He no longer sports the beard or the mustache and his lips look exposed, vulnerable.

He says, "You look terrific," and looks from the short denim skirt that shows off my legs to my straight shoulder-length hair that appears as blond as before. What he cannot see is the black lace bra and thong I have bought for the occasion. The thong rides up uncomfortably between my buttocks as I sway a little and tell him I know a good place for dinner—a place where I know I won't know anyone.

It is in the Latin Quarter, crowded with noisy students, and filled with smoke. There are red-checked tablecloths and candles, and the *patronne* wears glasses and a gray dress and looks like a school teacher. She stares disapprovingly. I expect her to say, *What are you doing here? Go home.*

He gazes blankly at the menu, hands it over to me, and says, "I suppose it's all good, hey? You order for us." I order a carafe of the house red and the *choucroute Alsacienne*. The waitress carries a heap of plates on a tray balanced against her flat stomach. She slaps the plates down while looking over her shoulder to answer someone else. She has brought the *boudin*, which I did not order. It always reminds me of what my mother called a private part: white and cylindrical and slightly shriveled. Michael smacks his lips and attacks it with gusto.

He tells me about his new wife—very beautiful, Irish. She was frightened by an animal scratching on the canvas tent. She thought it was a lion and screamed. It was only an anteater looking for eggs, but by the time she had found that out the Great White Hunter was in her bed.

"What *is* this I'm eating?" he asks me suddenly, chewing slowly and looking down at his *boudin*.

"It's a French dish," I say vaguely, plunging into mine, after all.

He goes on talking about his new wife, so I say nothing about my husband's new mistress. "She's barely twenty-three. Can you imagine?" and he makes the gesture that conveys voluptuous curves.

I ask why the wife has not accompanied him on this trip, and he explains that there is a baby at home. "A *baby*," I say and shift on my seat. The thong rides up between my buttocks again.

He says his wife has the fiery temper that is said to go with the Irish background, and when she drinks too much, she throws things. "She once threw a glass of passion fruit juice right into my face," he says and gulps more wine, staining his soft lips black.

When he tries to pay the check he realizes he has forgotten his credit card.

Outside it is raining softly, and everything shimmers. Raindrops hang down from the chestnut trees like tinsel. He suggests we take a walk to see the city. "You'll get your feet wet," I say, looking at his thin, yellow canvas shoes.

He thinks that funny. He opens the umbrella I have learned to take with me in Paris, but he holds it more over his head than mine, so that the water trickles down my neck, and my hair begins to curl.

"Maybe we should get a taxi and just drive around," I suggest. Still it takes a while to find a taxi, and by then my shoes are soaked.

He tells the driver to go down the Champs Élysées, which he pronounces as though it rhymes with lamp and lice. The driver turns his head and peers at him and says, "Où?"

"Doesn't he know his city?" he says to me, as I explain. The driver starts off so abruptly we are thrown back into our seats, but then slows down immediately and wants to know where exactly on the Champs Élysées we wish to go. "I don't know. Just drive down the street, can't you?" Michael says in his schoolboy French. *"Conduisez! Conduisez!"* he says loudly. "Is that too much to ask?"

The driver is heading toward the Champs Élysées shouting that he will drive us anywhere, he will drive us to hell.

"Stop the car immediately!" Michael leans forward and tells the driver that he has never met anyone so rude in his life, that the French people are all rude, most of all when they get into a car. *"Le peuple le plus impoli dans le monde!"* he shouts, his anger fueling this sudden surge of French.

The driver stops the cab so fast, we both fall forward from our seats.

We are at the Étoile, in the midst of heavy traffic under driving rain. The driver gets out and stretches to his full height. I hang onto Michael's arm, but he shakes me off and gets out of the taxi, too. He was never big as a Great White Hunter, but he seems suddenly to have shrunk standing on the sidewalk of this city in the rain. The driver is probably as young as Michael's young new wife. The two men size one another up. I step out of the taxi and say, "Let's just pay the fare and go." The rain falls on my hair, my face, my shoulders.

The driver shouts, "Dirty foreigner!" and spits into the water that rushes down the gutter.

"The French don't like it if you don't pay what you owe," I say and open up my purse and take out some bills. The Great White Hunter holds onto my money, and the driver pulls it away. The driver pushes him, and he falls sideward on his leg and his hands in the gutter where the water rushes down the street. The money drops into the water, and the driver scoops it up. Michael shouts for the police, as the taxi driver drives away with my money.

We are on the edge of the Avenue de la Grande Armee. Rain falls, and the cars spray our clothes. My hair tumbles in my face. My shirt clings to my breasts. My denim skirt feels heavy. The thong cuts into my flesh. I ask, "Are you all right?" as I help Michael to his feet.

"Having the time of my life," he says.

"I had better take you back to your hotel," I say.

We hail another taxi. I give the directions this time and take out a handkerchief and wipe my face and the Great White Hunter's wounds. We drive to the hotel in silence. I help him out and into the small lobby of the hotel. In the dim light, I look around the seedy place. It smells of cabbage. The concierge stares at us.

"I think I had better go," I say.

"A shower?" he suggests.

"Another time, perhaps," I say.

"Come on, I need your help," he urges and hands me his heavy metal key.

The iron door of the elevator closes like a concertina. He leans on me and hobbles down the corridor, though he seems hardly wounded. We stagger into his small room with its narrow bed, orange cotton bedspread and a long thin bolster for a pillow. There is a basin behind a screen where I help him wash his hands. "Take off your trousers and let me look at your knee," I say. I wash his cut knee. His legs are striped white and brown where he has worn shorts and high socks in the sun. He throws himself down on his back with his knees across the end of the bed and his calves dangling. He stares up at the ceiling, his arms folded behind his head. His underwear gapes slightly, and I catch a glimpse of his penis. He says, "Fuck," and then he sort of snorts and says, "She left."

"What are you talking about?" I ask.

"My wife. I'm talking about my goddam wife."

I ask, "She really left you?" and take off my wet shoes and wiggle my toes on the bare floor.

He says, "Yes, well," and looks up at my legs and adds, "We had a fight, and she left."

I say, "She did?" and sit down on the bed and put my hand on his broad shoulder with sympathy. I say, "Well, if it's any consolation, my husband has taken a mistress," and take off my wet shirt.

He considers my breasts in my black lace bra and says, "The bastard, the fucking bastard—doesn't know a good thing when he sees one."

"How could your wife leave *you*?" I ask and shake my head in disbelief.

"The goddam bitch just got up and took the baby and all the furniture and walked out."

I say, "God, just like that! What a cruel thing to do. When you came back from safari, everything was gone?"

He nods and says, "Everything, everything I own."

I tell him how sorry I am and slip out of the denim skirt and sit there in the black lace bra and thong. He smiles and his eyes look very blue.

He sits up and says, "Hey, I didn't know you were still in love with me."

"Neither did I," I say.

He leans across the bed and puts his finger into the black elastic of the thong. He says, "What's this?" His lips are slightly open. I can hear the sound of the rain falling as he leans toward me.

The Adulterous Woman

Anna carried the distinctive light blue box from the famous jewelry store onto the airplane. It was heavy, and as she lifted it to place it in the overhead bin, the man in the seat beside her rose to help.

"May I?" he said.

"That's quite all right," she replied quickly and glanced at him, a large, blond, ruddy-faced man who looked at her hopefully. She closed the overhead bin with a loud snap.

The man appeared never to have traveled before, as he kept asking her how to move his seat or attach the headphones to listen to the music. He told her it was his first time in Rome and wanted to know if it would be worth his while to spend the day there, or if she deemed it wiser to wait at the airport during the stopover. Anna said she was going into Rome for the day, herself, and added, "But it may be very crowded, because of Easter," and shut her eyes to shut him out. She slept fitfully, disturbed by the jostling of the plane as it bounced about in currents of air, and by the man's arm, his leg. She tried to nudge his arm to one side, to shift her legs, but each time she moved away from him, he moved closer to her, so that his leg pressed against hers once again.

Anna wanted to tell him she was not alone, had been married for many years to a good man, a doctor, who loved her. They had always been faithful to one another, had cared for one another in times of trouble and sickness, but instead she gave the man's thick arm a vicious jab with her elbow, so that he retreated slightly, blinked his white eyelashes at her, and gave her a reproachful glance. Then he renewed his attack. After a while, exhausted, she gave up and fell asleep with his thick leg pressing against hers.

She dreamt of her dead sister: saw her descending from the sky, sitting in a sort of garlanded throne. Someone was telling Anna to speak to her only sister for the last time, to say her last words, but when the throne approached, and Anna reached up to hold her sister in her arms, she saw the blood and the horribly mangled body and recoiled unable to think of anything to say.

When she woke, her mouth dry, her limbs aching, she rose and stretched up and felt around in the bin above in the dark, making sure that the light blue box with its expensive silver gift for her nephew was still there.

The ruddy-faced man kept moving his leg against hers. She gave him a little kick with her high heel. She wanted to explain that she was making this long trip out to South Africa for her nephew's wedding, that she was going back to the place where she was born, a place she had not wanted to visit for many years. She was making this expensive voyage on her own to attend the wedding of her dead sister's only boy, that she needed to concentrate on the reading he had asked her to make in the church.

At first she had refused, saying she could not possibly do such a thing. He had said, "But you and Mum were always reading stuff in church. She told me you were both chapel prefects, that you did the flowers, sang in the choir."

She remembered all the hours she and her only sister had spent in the muted light of the school chapel: she saw them stepping back from the altar, standing side-by-side to survey their arrangements of flowers with a critical eye, making sure they were identical in their twin silver flutes on the altar. She recalled the blue runner on the chapel floor, the narrow stained-glass windows, the scent of incense, the Magnificat sung in the wooden choir stalls in white dresses, their eyes turned back in ecstasy.

"I don't want to read that passage they always read at weddings about Charity," she found herself telling her nephew.

"You don't have to read that," he said. She had consented to read something secular, instead: she had decided on lines from Spenser's Prothalamion with the refrain, "Sweet Thames! Run softly 'til I end my song," but she thought now that the rivers out there did not run softly but dry between cracked banks.

And, really, what could one say about the state of matrimony? Sometimes, as she talked to her busy husband and watched his restless gaze wander from her face to the clock, she thought of it as synonymous with solitude. She lay awake in the dark, listening to the droning of the engines, twisting and turning in the narrow cramped space beside the large man in the window seat. The plane rolled and dipped, and the seat belt sign remained lit. A steward bent over her seat and offered her a glass of lemonade. She felt as if she had been traveling through the dark night forever.

At dawn when the plane finally landed in Rome, with a grinding roar, shuddering and shaking, the objects shifting and the doors to the overhead bins flying open, she rose fast, took down her precious burden, and hurried off the plane, glancing over her shoulder to make sure the ruddy-faced man was not following her.

She checked her suitcase at the baggage counter in the airport and asked if she could leave her gift as well, but the man, who wore a bandage over one eye, squinted at the blue box and shook his head. He said he could not guard a package of that kind.

She climbed up the steps of the train and looked around warily at the people already seated there. She found a seat by a window, and put the light-blue box between her legs. She should have covered it over with brown paper, she thought.

It was early, the sky still a faint pink. The compartment was nearly empty. A man and woman, husband and wife, Anna was sure, sat facing one another on the other side of the compartment. The man was murmuring strangely—surely madly to himself, she thought, while the pale woman looked out of the window and never replied, her mouth dipping sulkily. Anna thought of the times she, too, had mumbled to herself, sitting beside a husband too distracted to listen. She thought of all the questions she had asked him, trying to drag him into a conversation. How hard it was for married people, even well-intentioned ones, to live side by side for years and years and not to treat one another with cruelty.

A young man in dark glasses and green trousers, his thick hair slicked back from his forehead, boarded and looked around the compartment. He came over to her and put his small green suitcase on the seat next to her. She wondered why he had chosen to sit there when so many seats were empty. She supposed it was because this seat was nearest the door, but his suitcase was small and appeared light. The man asked her to watch it for a moment, because he had forgotten to punch his ticket.

"Oh, do you have to punch your ticket? I didn't punch mine either," she said, taking her own ticket out of her pocket and wondering how the young man could be so sure she was sufficiently trustworthy to guard his suitcase. He plucked her ticket out of her hand before she could protest, and said, "I'll do it for you," rushing off down the steps.

She waited as the compartment filled up, wondering when the man would come back, and what she should do if he did not. Surely he would claim his suitcase, she thought, looking at the small green bag on the seat. What if the man did not return? Would she be fined if she were found without a ticket? Could she be put in jail? She looked nervously down the aisle to see if there were a conductor on the train. Did the man do this for a living, she wondered, carrying off tickets from unsuspecting tourists? But then, what about his suitcase? Perhaps there was nothing precious inside. Perhaps he would not mind if his suitcase were carried away without him?

The man returned and sat down next to her, giving her back her ticket and smiling. She felt he was staring at her intensely from behind his dark glasses and shifting his narrow hips. She wondered what he was thinking.

She thought of coming to Rome at Easter with her sister and staying in the hotel at the top of the Spanish steps. They had walked down the steps to the boat-shaped fountain below and then through the streets in the glare of spring light. Her sister had spoken of her unhappy marriage, her husband's infidelity, his violence. She had told her she only had one life to live, and she should enjoy it. "Carpe diem," she had exhorted, and looked up at the swallows turning in the blue sky and at the long-stemmed pine trees and the ocher walls of the ancient buildings. She had listened to the bells ringing, calling the faithful to celebrate the risen Christ.

She remembered how she and her sister had bought silk underwear in a shop on the Via Condotti, identical but for the colors, hers white and her sister's, pink. Later, she had received a letter from her sister telling her of her meeting with a man in Istanbul at the airport, and of her love affair.

The man in the dark glasses had leaned forward to pick up his suitcase, letting his hand brush against her arm. She rose abruptly and left the train at the next stop, carrying her box with her through the crowds in the station, clutched to her chest. She wandered through the early morning streets of Rome. The Romans had all left, it seemed, and there were only Christian pilgrims come from all parts of the world, roaming through the streets of the city in large groups, covering their heads as they stepped from the light into the dark of churches, going to mass.

She returned to the familiar places she and her sister had visited: the Bernini fountains, the Borghese museum, staring at the marble statues. She lingered in the cool of the gardens, fragrant with pine. She walked down the Via Veneto, looking into the windows of shut-up shops. She passed the restaurants with outdoor tables, yellow tablecloths and bouquets of spring flowers, where families already congregated.

It was growing hotter, the noonday sun high and bright. Her feet ached in her high-heeled shoes from all the walking. She was growing hungry. Her head felt light from her sleepless voyage through the night.

She remembered coming home from boarding school with her sister at Easter and eating a huge meal at the round table with the hand-crocheted tablecloth. She saw herself and her sister dancing around the table to the strains of "The Graduation Ball," her hand around her sister's slender waist, turning and turning, laughing, their full mauve skirts rising around them, their white petticoats visible at the edges like foam. She saw the sideboard laden with food: the roasted lamb, the crispy potatoes, the gem squash, butter melting in the hollow halves, the bowl of bright tropical fruit: mangoes, pomegranates and lichees, the trifle topped with whipped cream, the chocolate Easter eggs.

She stood at the edge of the Trevi fountain and listened to the sound of the water falling. She walked as far as the Pantheon and stared up at its vast dome. Her arms ached from carrying the blue box, her gift for her sister's boy and his bride.

She heard the bells ringing and the singing from the street, and felt that fate had guided her random footsteps. She went in and found a space in the crowded Anglican church near the altar, slipping in behind a stone column and standing close beside an African man who glanced at her and smiled, as if welcoming her. They stood side by side, their black and white hands holding the same book, as she had never been able to do in her home as a child. They prayed the same prayers and sang the familiar melodies together. The African sang loudly and well, and emboldened by his example, she, too, lifted up her voice.

There were many Africans in the church, all dressed in their finery, visiting the city for Easter. The church was fragrant with incense and the strong cloying scent of lilies and the warm perfumed skins of so many faithful come to celebrate the resurrection of Christ. Big bowls of peonies and foxgloves and lilies stood by the altar. There was deep silence as the people knelt and bowed their heads and prayed.

Leaning against the pew, on her knees, she stared up at the figure of the risen Christ above the altar, in his cloud of glory, his arms outstretched, his knees twisted to one side in his gold robes. She closed her eyes and prayed for her sister's only boy, whom his dead mother had loved so much, and who was about to embark so bravely, so recklessly, knowing what he knew, into matrimony.

When the large congregation rose like a wave, surging up the aisle, a glad throng of singing souls, she hesitated. Should she leave the church without partaking of the body and blood of Christ on this most holy of days? Could she walk up the aisle with the distinctive light blue box dangling from her arm and thus burdened, weighed down, and flaunting this symbol of wealth and privilege, lift her hands to receive the wafer and tilt the cup of wine to her lips? Did she dare abandon the precious gift, leaving it lying unguarded beside this dark stranger?

She thought of her sister's boy, her blue-eyed, honey-haired nephew, and how much he resembled his mother, so that every time he pursed his lips, she saw her dead sister as a young girl standing before the mirror and pursing her lips and giggling and pretending to be Brigitte Bardot.

She glanced again at the man beside her. He was dressed in a sweater which looked as though it had been washed so often it had shrunk, and light brown shoes which clashed with his navy pants. He had a broad, flat face and tranquil eyes, which shone in the light coming in through the stained-glass windows in slanting rays. He appeared tired—the service must have started much earlier, she realized—or perhaps even bored with the long, sung Eucharist, yawning from time to time and shifting about in his seat and glancing at her. He watched her, with, she thought, a glint of amusement in his eyes. She felt he knew what she was thinking.

Was he a good man who had risen early and come a long way to attend this sung mass? Or was he an idle passer-by who had happened to wander into the church and was looking around for just such an unsuspecting tourist as she? Was he planning to rush off down the aisle and disappear into the crowd, carrying away her precious gift?

The bells rang; the singing rose. "Nearer my God to Thee, nearer to Thee," the faithful sang. The black priest in his splendid white Easter robes lifted his arms to bless the host. The censers clacked, sliding up and down on their chains, and the incense rose. She breathed it in with fervor. The gold of Christ's pierced flesh shone above.

She thought of her sister's last moments as her husband drove the car fast through the dark into the ramp at the side of the road. Did she realize she was going to die as she pressed her arms and feet against the dashboard and the floor? Did she feel her wrists and ankles snapping as the car crashed?

A cold sweat moistened her brow, and her head spun. She pushed the blue box forward under the pew and stood, buoyed up by the singing, carried forward by the crowd. She stepped out into the aisle, glancing behind her, and catching sight of the blue box protruding visibly from under the pew, lying as if abandoned on the floor. She was in the long line of communicants, her hands folded before her in prayer. She was no longer able to retrace her steps, swept along by the singing, joyful crowd. She, too, sang.

She knelt at the altar, took the host into her trembling, outstretched hands. She swallowed the wine voluptuously, a little running down her chin. Her heart beat faster and faster, and her whole body pressed against the altar rail as she strained toward the risen Christ. She saw his golden face twisted close to her own as if he were about to cry out to her.

The light was in her eyes like water. In a daze, breathing deeply, she forgot her nephew's wedding, her murdered sister, her long voyage through the night, her husband of many years. It seemed to her that Christ had covered her over as she leaned back from the altar, the cold stone against her knees.

Baboons

As they drive along the road to Oudtshoorn and draw near the house where the dinner is being held, Jan Marais tells his wife Kate that he is having an affair with Serge, his anesthetist.

Jan draws the car—the black Mercedes convertible his mother-in-law gave them as a wedding present—over onto the shoulder of the road, anticipating Kate's response. He wants to stop so that, if necessary, he can put his arms around his wife's shoulders and comfort her, should she weep in the car. The top is down, and Jan can see a small troop of brown-gray baboons by the side of the road. Big males and two or three smaller females with several young baboons around them are sitting on rocks or rooting in the earth under the wild fig and thorn trees. The sultry heat of the December evening is tempered only by the wind, which blows the branches about wildly.

Jan turns off the engine and the lights, but leaves the radio playing. A woman is singing softly: "Take me to your heart again…" Jan looks at his wife and waits for her reply, but she seems to be looking at the baboons.

"Baboons," she says incongruously, as though this were some sort of reply to what he has told her. Why can the woman not concentrate on the matter at hand? Jan thinks. This is one of the things which annoys him about Kate: the way she flits from subject to subject without any connection, the way she dithers, never able to make up her mind. He feels it is having an effect on him, on his work, where prompt decisions are a matter of life and death.

Kate is sitting beside him with her small hands in her lap, staring at the baboons. He notices how nicely the blue of her flowered dress reflects her star-shaped sapphire earrings. Kate has a way with color. She knows how to dress with understated elegance. He sees how flat the collar of this dress lies against her smooth white neck. She holds her small, dark head erect, and her lips turn down ever so slightly at the edges. Even in the fading light of day, he can see how her brown eyes glimmer in a hazy, dreamy way. He sees her luminous skin, the soft tinge in the cheeks which rises from her neck like a promise, and he smells her sweet odor of verbena and roses.

He asks her, "Don't you have anything to say?" but she does not answer.

Jan met Kate at a university party two years ago. When Jan left the small *dorp* in the Free State, where there is nothing much but dust and heat, to go to university in Cape Town to study medicine, his family was afraid he might marry a rich girl, and they would never see him again. But they have seen him more frequently since he married Kate, who often invites them to stay in their big house. Jan's mother, a clever woman, is from a French Huguenot family, the du Toits, and plays the organ in the Dutch Reformed Church. When Jan was a boy, he would sit by her side and pump the organ.

Now he sits beside his wife, Kate, in the black Mercedes with the tan leather seats and the stick shift. He waits in the humid heat for her to say something, but she says nothing.

Besides the low voice on the radio and the barking of the baboons, there is only the lonely sigh of the wind in the branches. Kate seems to be gazing dreamily into the tangle of the wild trees.

Kate is not saying anything, because her head is spinning. The tan leather of the car, the thick, dark mass of the trees, and the brown-gray bodies of the baboons with their dog-like muzzles are all spinning around her, alarmingly. For one terrifying moment, she has the sensation of leaving her body, abandoning herself; she can see herself from some distance: a pale woman with short, dark curls, sitting strangely still in a car.

As a child she sometimes felt this when she lay in the long dormitory at her Anglican boarding school near Cape Town. The narrow beds and the bare, whitewashed walls of the room would spin around her, and she would feel she was leaving herself behind. Sometimes she would say the prayer she had learned as a child: "Matthew, Mark, Luke, and John, God bless the bed that I lie on," and she would come back to herself. And there have been other moments in her life when she is not quite sure if she was dreaming or not.

Now she feels she must say something, anything, in response to what Jan has told her, if she is going to reclaim her discarded body, if she is to stop herself from floating out into the twilight. What comes to her from a distance is something in French, which Jan does not speak. She says, in her calm, gentle voice, *Tout lasse, tout passe, tout casse.*

* * *

Kate was studying art and languages at Cape Town University when she first met Jan. She liked his blond good looks, his good brain, and his frank and sometimes tactless manner, the way he said what he thought. Kate was taught as a child not to say things unless they were pleasant. She liked the fact that Jan was poor and from such a big family, and particularly that he was an Afrikaner, perhaps because it annoyed her widowed mother so much.

"You are all I have in the world now, darling," her mother said to Kate, her only child, when her husband died. During her studies at university, Kate continued to go home for the holidays, to drive her mother to church on Sundays, to sit and knit with her in the chintz-covered armchairs in the evenings, to fix her drink, and to go out to dinner at her mother's dull friends' houses, where no one ever said anything unpleasant.

Still, when Kate told her about Jan, her mother said, "Over my dead body will you marry a Boer!"

"Mother!" Kate said, appalled.

Her mother sighed and put her knitting needles down in her lap and said, more mildly, "He comes from such a different background, darling."

"That's why I like him," Kate said, rudely.

This altercation, highly unusual for Kate and her mother, may have strengthened Kate's resolve to marry Jan. Kate has her stubborn side.

Also, Kate liked the fact that Jan was studying to be a thoracic surgeon, that he would be saving lives. Kate herself has saved lives, though only those of a few wounded birds, two stray cats, a monkey which followed her around the garden for a while, before it turned vicious and bit her, and a puppy she once found half-drowned in a ditch.

Of course, Kate had not realized the long hours required to save lives, or she might have been less enthusiastic about Jan's work. She hadn't realized that Jan would come home late every night, his face gray, and so exhausted that all he could do was to throw himself, unwashed, smelling of sweat, into the big white bed where he slept as though nothing could wake him. She hadn't realized that he would be gone when she woke every morning, leaving the long corridors, the wide terrace, the smooth green lawn empty.

Jan says harshly, "What did you say? What! What does that mean?" He is sweating slightly, and it seems to him that the sultry summer evening is growing warmer rather than cooler. Even the wind seems to be abating. Jan hates it when Kate speaks French or worse still, Italian, which seems affected to him. He hates the way she claps after a concert, lifting high her small hands and shouting out not "Bravo!" like everyone else but "Bravi!"

Jan speaks only English and Afrikaans. A scholarship boy, and captain of the rugby team, Jan was always first in his class, and the first in his family to go on to university. His father held a minor position on the South African railways, until he was dismissed because of something he did to a black man.

Besides, Jan doesn't understand how anyone would want to speak French at an important moment like this. He imagines Kate has said something condescendingly polite, which she often does, something calm and reassuring, when he is in a rage, in her low melodious English voice, something that by contrast reminds him all too well how his mother suddenly screamed at his father or at one of his little brothers or sisters in Afrikaans, or even at him, Jan, her pet, suddenly turning on him with cruelty, lashing out at him. It reminds him all too well how his mother would stride through their narrow house on a rampage, swiping with the hairbrush at any exposed limb or posterior in sight.

He turns his face toward Kate in the half-dark and asks again what she meant, but she does not bother to translate her foreign words. When she does not respond, he leans forward over the shiny wooden steering wheel, embracing it, clinging to it for support. He says, "I couldn't go on lying to you. I hate to lie to you. You cannot imagine how lonely it is to have to lie. I had to tell you the truth. And Serge will be there tonight. I've promised him I'll spend a weekend with him, so that we can sort this all out." He stops to wait for some response, but when Kate again says nothing, he goes on. "It has really no importance at all, to you and me, you understand. It doesn't mean anything has changed between us, that I don't love you still, which I do."

It is at that moment that the radio, which has been playing, goes off abruptly, and there is dead silence in the car.

Having said something to Jan, even if it was in French, and hearing Jan respond, saying something about love, Kate is now able to realize she is sitting there beside him in the car, slumped over a little, her hands still in her lap, the baboons on the rocks under the trees, the wind blowing her hair in her face.

She is thinking of what she wrote in her diary this morning. Kate keeps a little, blue leather diary diligently, as she does everything else. The people at the photography gallery where she works in Cape Town appreciate her diligence, her punctuality, her tact with their difficult clients, and her quiet unobtrusive presence. Her voice on the telephone is praised particularly. In her diary she writes down her weight, what exercise she has taken, what she has eaten (she tries to eat only fruit, vegetables, and whole-wheat grains), how many photographs she has sold for the gallery, a record of her periods, and, from time to time, even adds a few words about the weather. Today, exceptionally, she has written: "ran to beach; porridge for breakfast and an apple; a wild blue sky; perhaps a baby? How wonderful!" She has not had her period for six weeks and three days.

She was planning to give Jan this news, when he gave her his own. She looks at him. She has always liked to stare at his startlingly handsome face: the tanned skin, the determined chin, high cheek bones, and slightly slanting, almost yellow eyes—eyes the same color as his hair. She wonders if she should say something about the baby, but it does not seem to be the right moment. Instead, Kate remembers something Jan has told her about his life, which she has never quite believed. When Jan was telling her this, she thought of what her mother says about Afrikaners, that they are too emotional, that they exaggerate. Her mother thinks Afrikaners are all hysterical.

Jan told Kate, one evening, when he had drunk a whole bottle of wine on the terrace, that as a boy, a teacher of his, an older man who taught him Latin, had fallen in love with him. "In love with you? A teacher?" she had said. Jan nodded and said the man had been exceptionally good to him and taken a particular interest in his work. He had even visited his home to convince his parents to let Jan go on to university, which they might not have done otherwise. He had helped him acquire the scholarship which enabled him to continue his studies. One evening, the man had invited him to his house, and Jan had asked him to "show him," was what Jan had actually said, about sex. "I wanted to seduce him," Jan said.

Kate had not really believed this story or certainly had never given it much importance. All the necessary details to make the story believable seemed to be missing. When she questioned Jan, he did not remember the essentials: where the man's house was, what he looked like, if he were old or young, or even whether the man had complied or not with Jan's request, or what had happened to him after that. "I think he got fired," Jan said, when she questioned him.

"You think?" she said, and he shrugged, smiled, and explained that it was like a dream where you don't remember what happens *after* you have fallen down the cliff.

Now Kate stares at Jan, trying to imagine him with Serge. He is wearing the cream silk shirt with the high collar and the Gucci loafers with the tassels Kate bought him for his birthday, which, she supposes, Serge admires.

Kate thinks of Serge and realizes with a shock that he looks a little like her: a tall, dark, curly-haired, athletic man, with a sensuous mouth, and ears that stick out slightly. He did his medical training with Jan. She remembers Jan telling her that Serge caught him once when he passed out the first time they had to dissect a cadaver. She also remembers Serge telling her he read all of Proust in seventy-eight hours. For a moment she sees Serge as she saw him the last time, walking down the hospital corridor in his white coat, swinging his hips slightly, waving a hand, and calling out to her and Jan, "See you."

What Kate wonders now is how she could have known Jan for two years and not been aware of what he was thinking or feeling to this extent, how she could have ignored something so basic about him. She has always felt that the sexual side of their relationship was satisfactory. There were moments in the night when Kate reached out, and he made love to her passionately. Is it possible for a man to love both men and women? she wants to ask him, but feels it would not be appropriate. But she is truly curious about such a phenomenon. She has the impression now that she knows nothing at all about this man, her husband, and perhaps the father of her unborn child. She is no longer even sure that his long absences, which she has always tolerated, were caused by his work. Was he perhaps with Serge? Were there others? Were there women as well as men?

At this moment, she hears a loud barking sound and looks at the baboons which seem to be quarreling. One of them, a larger one with a dark muzzle, is baring its long teeth. A smaller, slender baboon leaves the troop and trots toward the car. It leaps easily and with surprising strength onto the bonnet of the car. The baboon lands lightly, its unsightly distended pink bottom lifted insolently, provocatively, toward their faces.

Jan blows the horn loudly and shouts out angrily, "Get off, Goddamn it!" and the baboon, startled, jumps down onto the side of the road. With measured gait, it trots slowly, importantly, across the twilit road, on its flat black hands, going toward the other side, pink bottom swinging and dark tail held upwards, and then, as though it were broken, falling downwards.

Kate watches anxiously, as the animal makes its way safely across the road. Then, for some reason, it stops and turns and stares back at their car. It seems to be looking at them with curiosity in the half-dark. Perhaps it thinks they have something to eat? Yet it holds something up to its mouth in almost human hands—is it a wild fig? Do baboons eat figs?

Kate remembers reading somewhere that baboons will eat animals and even attack a small antelope. They are stronger than they look, apparently. This one appears to be nibbling on something. Then calmly it returns, going back from whence it came, going back to join its mates, who are barking in the dark thicket of the trees. As it crosses the road this second time, it is not as lucky. Though the baboon moves more quickly, a big blue car comes careening around the corner, and the animal, caught in its high beams, stops transfixed for a second too long, and is thrown brutally to one side.

Kate cries out loudly, "Oh no!" and puts her hands to her mouth and makes a little high-pitched sob.

Jan thinks that if she had said these words in response to his initial statement, if she had sobbed instead of speaking French, if the baboon had not jumped onto the bonnet of his car, he would probably have taken her into his arms, and things would not have gone any further.

Instead, he turns to her and hits her hard across her small, open mouth. He hits her with the back of his hand, so that his knuckles slam against her open lips, and he can feel her teeth. For a moment he thinks he might have dislodged one of them.

It is not the first time he has hit Kate in a moment of uncontrollable rage. Once, he had come in very late for dinner, after operating on a small boy. The child had bubble gum caught in his windpipe and lay on the operating table, gasping for breath. Jan had hesitated too long over an essential move, distracted for a second by something—the child's blond curls clinging to his white forehead, his little beating heart, and he had lost the boy's life. When Kate came out onto the terrace to greet him in her perfect pink dress, her single string of pearls, her dark curls fluffed up adorably around her pink cheeks, and complained about Jan's tardy arrival, he had simply hit her across her pretty face and left her standing there.

A placid, gentle woman, Kate, too, is capable of passion at unexpected moments. She is a surprisingly eager lover in his bed. Once, they had been at a party at the hospital, and she had drunk too much cheap wine. Waiting for the elevator, as they were leaving, Kate said, "I *saw* you putting your hand on that fat woman's leg," referring to one of his favorite night nurses, a good-humored, big-breasted Afrikaans nurse, who was sweating in her tight silk dress. Kate had hit Jan across the cheek, hard.

Now Kate takes out a tissue from her sequined handbag and spits a tooth into the kleenex and wipes the blood from her mouth. She says, "My tooth!" in an anguished tone, and he can see the tears in her dark eyes. Now, Jan thinks, she will weep as she should.

Jan feels suddenly calmer and for some reason, optimistic. Everything will work out with time, he thinks. Now that Kate knows about Serge, now that he has hit her, that she has even lost a tooth, he feels a certain relief. His hand throbs from the blow against her teeth which worries him somewhat, and he massages his knuckles, which hurt. His hands are very important to him, of course. He does not feel sorry for Kate at all, though he notices there is blood spattered on her blue dress, and he realizes they will not be able to go to the party now. So much the better, he thinks. The party was never a good idea.

Though she has lost a tooth and tastes the blood in her mouth, though she feels her smarting lips and her throbbing gums, for a moment Kate is not absolutely certain that Jan has hit her. It does not seem possible. She can see no reason why he would have. She is the injured party, after all. What has she done to him? She thinks of the numerous advantages his marriage has conferred on him: the big white house with the tennis court and the smooth green lawns, the servants who cook and tend the garden and press his clothes, the important people she has introduced him to, even his job at the hospital, which was procured mainly because her mother knew the head of the department. She thinks of all the lavish affection she showers on him daily: the big bowls of flowers she arranges in his study, the clothes she buys him, the bills she pays, the nights she has sat up in the dusk, nibbling on nuts and sipping sweet sherry, waiting for him to come home, or, even worse, when he is home, watching him gulp down the fresh grilled fish and the healthful salads she has had prepared, in silence in the half-dark on the terrace, with only the sound of the crickets shrilling in the thick shrubbery and the candles flickering in the wind.

She wants to ask Jan if he regrets what he has done, if he is sorry for the harm he has caused her. But instead she looks at her tooth in the tissue and makes a tremendous effort to think of something that would comfort her.

Then she notices the poor baboon, which is making little pitiful cries at the side of the road. It has staggered up and seems confused, as if it has lost its way. It seems to want to cross the road. "Oh, help, please, look, it's alive!" she says impulsively, following her heart.

Jan glances at her with impatience and shakes his head, but he throws open the door of the car and jumps out into the warm night air. Besides, he is glad to be out of the car and away from her, glad to stretch his legs. He walks slowly along the side of the road in the darkness toward the animal. He stands with his hands in his pockets, kicks at the loose dirt, and peers down at the wounded baboon on the ground. He considers. He is not sure what to do about it. Probably better to put it out of its misery, he thinks, but remembers something about not touching a wounded animal. This one is probably a female, he thinks, and her young are near, though the rest of the troop seem to have scattered into the bush. He notices the arm of the baboon, which hangs pitifully broken and bleeding from its shoulder. He crouches down to observe.

It is turning almost completely dark now, the sun already beneath the horizon, only faint traces of pink remaining in the sky. He cannot see very clearly. He hears the crickets shrilling, as he stares down at the wounded animal, leaning a little closer to get a better look at the coarse, matted hair, the bleeding arm. The animal moves with such sudden speed and in such an unforeseen manner that Jan is unable to react. With its one good arm it reaches up and claws at him, tearing away the skin and the flesh from his shoulder so that it hangs down horribly.

Then Jan hears something else, the familiar sound of the Mercedes' engine revving up, and he is caught in the bright headlights. He staggers up into the road, transfixed, his hand to his bleeding shoulder, holding onto his flesh. As the car comes toward him, for a moment he thinks of Serge. Then he starts to spin, leaving his body behind, floating out into the dark.

Lunch with Mother

I t was my habit in those days to lunch with Mother every Sunday. She lives near the boys' school I had attended for that reason. My father was missing in action, when I was a baby, you see. His family, wealthy English people, devastated by his early death, gave my mother a generous allowance with the proviso that we would visit, which we did yearly. Mother moved back to Johannesburg, bought a Dutch-gabled house with a lovely view and a terraced garden.

This Sunday luncheon, October third—I remember the date because it was my thirtieth birthday—I entered the iron gates in my old Morris, somewhat late. I had forgotten my car keys on the desk in my flat on the fifth floor and had to climb back upstairs to fetch them. It was also shortly after I had lost my position in the boys' school where I had taught history, something I had not mentioned to Mother.

Coming up her steep graveled driveway with its flowers—I can never remember the names of flowers—on either side, I noticed a silver-blue Lancia near the house. I wondered—Mother's friends are not the kind of people with whom I usually mix—who the visitor might be. Our luncheons were *en tête-à-tête*. As Mother said, if her son was only going to trouble himself to visit once a week, she wanted him all to herself.

She had been disappointed when I decided to do my master's at Cape Town rather than Wits, and even more disappointed when, on completing my degree, I had found a flat in Hillbrow and acquired my second-hand Morris to drive to Bedford View where I taught history to the boys in standard six.

"But you could have had a whole wing to yourself here!" Mother had protested when I told her I was not coming back home. I wanted to suggest, as I had several times, awkward bookish boy that I was, that she remarried, to which she always replied, "What do I want with some old boy!" as though that were her only choice. Several suitors, many of them young and attractive, had sat around our lounge longingly. Mother had seriously considered an English lord who smoked a pipe, but in the end proclaimed he was another fortune hunter. I suspect she liked her independence.

What she added, to persuade me to move back, was, "I wouldn't bother you at all, darling. Wilson could drive you to school in the Humber Super Snipe. You could bring home anyone you wanted," which was not the case. Mother took an instant dislike to anyone close to me.

As I called Mother's name in the dark hallway, with its stable door, old kist, grandfather clock, the bowl of proteas in the soup tureen, and the smell of some delicious dish, some slightly sweet favorite from my childhood, I presumed, I was startled by a slender young woman who emerged from Mother's study. She told me Mother was in the garden in a low voice, her words clipped, her pronunciation English. She explained that she had been engaged to help with the accounts and gave me a limp handshake, her pink hand slightly damp and hot.

When mother had bought the house, she had hired enough staff to man a ship: at least six house servants, and four or five men in the garden—not all that unusual in that time and place: Johannesburg in the forties. The cook, a large cheerful woman with a great sense of humor, the only person who still calls me Petrel, after the bird, remained with us for years. An ancient Zulu washerwoman came once a week to wash and iron. The rest of the staff, various black nannies and manservants, who took care of me, cleaned the large house and served at table, changed frequently. Mother was a demanding employer and never entirely satisfied with her servants or, I sometimes felt, with me.

She rarely hired young women, preferring older ones or men, who, according to her, were less trouble. I thought this woman, her thin fair hair lying loose and shiny on her shoulders, might have been twenty-five or even younger. Of course, she was white, not in uniform, and apparently in a secretarial position.

She stood erect in a tight-fitting black, polo-necked shirt and a dark, short skirt which exposed her thin, slightly bandy legs. A little pink in the face, she gave off a faint odor of eau de cologne and perspiration which conveyed an idea of panic. I remember thinking she was not the type to last long with Mother.

As I walked out into the garden, the sun in my eyes, I heard her say, to my surprise, "Happy birthday." I turned to thank her, but she had vanished through the swing doors into the kitchen. All that was left was the sound of the doors swinging, the clack of dishes, the muffled laughter and the delicious smell of cooking.

For a moment, I was tempted to go into the kitchen and find out what was funny. I had spent long afternoons there as a boy on my return from school, when I often found mother in her darkened room, taking her siesta, which sometimes extended until evening, her damp silk gown hardly covering her heavy breasts, her mouth slightly open, her dark curls clinging to her forehead, one arm flung over her face.

I would remove my lace-up shoes, socks, and tie and sit at the kitchen table, elbows on the pine, a glass of lemonade and a thick slice of coconut cake with white icing before me, basking in the smells of stewing servants' meat bubbling in thin pots on the stove, the banter and the jokes in different tongues. A male visitor often perched on a stool, legs apart, hat in his hands, bringing news from the homeland; man servants chopped and stirred, and our large cook presided proudly over her domain with a white *doek* around her head.

I had learned some Zulu and a fair amount of Xhosa from the servants who came and went. Mother, though devoted, never spent much time with me. She always suffered from delicate health and consequently led an indolent life— breakfasted late in bed; rarely came downstairs until late afternoon when she reclined languidly on her day bed on the sleeping porch, or out in the garden listening to the sound of the wind in the palm trees, embroidering or reading or just dreaming. Occasionally, when I would beg her to as a boy, she would sit in her loose gown at the grand piano in the drawing room, and I would climb onto the stool beside her as she played one of Chopin's slow mazurkas, often breaking off in the middle of a chord with a sigh. She liked to go out at night for cocktails or dinner or, occasionally, had friends to dine.

She often complained of insomnia, rose at odd hours and wandered around the house half-naked, not bothering, in the heat and with the servants in their quarters, to dress.

She had a strange attitude toward her body, as though *her* body could not be associated with anything sexual, and therefore did not need to be covered. She would often sit at her dressing table with only her thin silk dressing gown, damp from her long bathing—she loved to linger in warm water— half open on her breasts, and have me brush her hair. I would stand behind her and brush until I was overwhelmed by the response of my body, young as I was, and would turn red and rush from the room. Once, I remember her teaching me how to kiss—I must have been fifteen or sixteen. She called it practicing. I remember my surprise and confusion at the dart of her tongue, her laughter.

Now, I dared not linger, knowing she was waiting. She was lounging in a deck chair reading under a tree, the mauve flowers falling softly around her. She reclined sideways in an attitude habitual to her, her head on her left hand, her little finger curved toward her lip. She sat up as she heard my step, let her book fall, and leaned toward me, stretching out both tiny, bejeweled hands.

All my life I have suffered from having a beautiful mother, so that when people meet me, they inevitably stare and say, "But you are Cecilia's son? You don't look like her at all!" And, of course, I don't: she is small and dark and every movement she makes, graceful; I am tall and fair and awkward. I take after Father in the photograph Mother keeps on her dressing table: a gawky young man punting under a bridge at Oxford, his pale hair and eyes and freckled skin melting into the sunlight, so that one notices above all the large hands, teeth, and ears.

At fifty, Mother was still so youthful-looking, she was often taken for my sister. It is the eyes that strike immediately: large and dark and softly shaded by heavy lashes. She is a fussy eater, finds the whole business of eating, as she says, tiresome, and she has remained slender, the dusky skin smooth. Seeing her sitting there lifting her handkerchief to dab at her damp upper lip, I could well imagine how my father must have found the young South African girl he had met one summer evening at an embassy party in London, irresistible. I remembered her once telling me, "Your father would do anything for me, anything."

A broad-brimmed straw hat dangled on the back of her chair, and today, perhaps because of my birthday, a gold locket my father had given her swung between her breasts in the opening of her cream organdy dress.

I could smell her heavy perfume long before she reached up to embrace me, brushing my cheek softly with her lips and whispering, "Happy birthday, darling. A big one, no? And I have a big surprise for you."

"The mystery guest?" I asked, wiping mauve lipstick from my cheek with my handkerchief. She blinked her eyes at me blankly. "The car in the driveway?" I explained.

"Lunch first," she replied coquettishly and let me help her rise, pressed me to her side softly, as we walked together in the dazzling, high-veld light. "Lovely, isn't it?" she said, looking around the garden, leaning on me and breathing somewhat heavily.

Perhaps because she takes so little exercise, or perhaps because of her tendency to asthma, any movement causes Mother to breathe heavily.

I remembered hearing her breathing in the corridor outside my room one night where I found her, her white body

glistening in the moonlight—I must have been about seven—
and stood staring up at her with a feeling of uneasiness, and
disturbance, mingled with a kind of admiration. She was
naked, rooting around in the linen closet, counting her sheets.
Not at all perturbed by my presence, she said in a cross voice,
"I am sure they are stealing my sheets," and led me back to
bed, bending over me, to kiss me good-night, her breasts
grazing my chest.

"Yes, lovely," I said, now, looking around.

It was spring, of course, the garden full of color: yellow and
white flowers mixed with mauve and dotted with fat, striped,
furry bees.

Mother then stared up at me with her penetrating gaze and
asked me how I was feeling, how my pupils were, how my
work had gone this week. I was not sure what to answer,
hoping to avoid the subject of my lost position, the scandal in
the school which had caused my dismissal.

Mother was always good at drawing people out, getting
them to confide their secrets. Not particularly given to
introspection, herself, she was nevertheless capable of taking a
brief but intense interest in the inner life of those around her,
though I've seen her get someone to reveal her deepest secrets,
with a few well-aimed questions, and then, once her victim
had left, complain how boring the woman was. "I'll never see
her again," Mother would say, with some satisfaction,
knowing the person, having confided all, would be too
ashamed to come back. A woman of intelligence and great
charm, Mother is particularly skillful at getting what she
wants from people.

However, I need not have worried about avoiding the
subject of my shame, at that point, for Mother, when I had
said something vague, had another in mind, though not

one I relished. She said, "We must have a little talk after luncheon, dear."

"About what, Mother?" I asked, somewhat anxiously.

"Business matters. Time you took a more active interest. I've managed it all for long enough. One of these days this will all belong to you." She made a wide trembling gesture toward the blue hills in the haze, her rings catching the light.

"Oh, Mother, you'll outlive me! Besides, I'd rather not think about all of that—my birthday, after all."

"That's exactly why we should think about it, darling. I need your help increasingly," she said and lowered her lashes mournfully for a moment.

I have never had much interest in money matters. On the contrary, just the mention of money makes my mind turn blank in a frightening fashion. I have never been good at mathematics, which puzzled my teachers and Mother, as I did well in other subjects, and Father had been gifted, had even wanted to be a mathematics professor.

Over the years, I had left all business to Mother. She had inherited my grandparents' money, had been lucky or astute or convincing in her business deals, had, indeed, as she reminded me from time to time, become wealthy. She would often say, "But Peter, darling, for heaven's sake, let me at least buy you a new jacket," twisting the arm of my old tweed jacket with its patched elbows, or lifting the cuff of a shirt to show its frayed edges. But I continued to live on my teacher's salary, and wear my old clothes.

"Now, Peter, at thirty you cannot avoid your responsibilities in this way," Mother scolded, as we went along the graveled path up to the house, side by side.

I said, "Please, not today. Besides, who knows what will happen out here," making a vague reference to the political situation, and walking so distractedly I almost stumbled over one of the gardeners, a young Xhosa who was crouched down weeding, near the path.

I may have failed to mention that I am short-sighted, and though I wear thick glasses, the here-and-now continues to come to me from a distance, as it were, through a blur, which is perhaps one of the reasons I have always preferred the past.

Mother, who was not always courteous with servants, shouted at the young man, "Jakob!" as though he were at fault. He lifted his head and his hand to shade his eyes; looked up at us and sprang erect and to one side, with one quick supple movement, and a rustle of his starched uniform, standing to his full height in the long khaki socks and shorts and shirt, all the gardeners wore.

Unusually tall and slim with dark, shiny skin, scars from some initiation ceremony, I presumed, ran slantwise across his prominent cheekbones. He held his neat head high and slightly to one side on a long neck, rather like a stiff exotic bud on a stem turning toward the sun. Like the secretary in the house, I had not seen him before.

For some reason, perhaps Mother's rudeness, I felt moved to speak to him, though I was not sure what to say. I looked around at the abundance of spring blooms nodding at his feet and found myself asking: "Jakob, would you pick some flowers for me—a big bunch? It's my birthday, and I would like to take them home, that is, if you don't mind, Mother?"

Before Mother could respond, the man nodded politely and said, as the young woman had done, "Happy birthday."

"Thank you," I said and gave him a smile. His teeth flashed in a wide frank response. At the same time, I thought I detected a rather sly, slightly amused expression in his dark gold, heavy-lidded eyes and sultry mouth.

Lunch with Mother

Mother drew me closer to her then, as though this request had pleased her. She often complained that I would accept nothing, had refused to take any of the delicate pieces of furniture from the house for my dark flat, or the elegant clothes or even jewelry: cuff links, gold chains, signet rings, it would be absurd to wear for the life I lead.

We went on up the path toward the house, Mother leaning on me, panting a little, the odor of cooking wafting from the kitchen. "Your favorite for lunch, today. Have you been eating enough, Peter? You're looking thin, a little anemic. Is there something on your mind, darling?" she asked me in her perspicacious way, staring at me intently and pressing my arm to her side.

For some reason, I remembered walking barefoot in the grass as a boy and being bitten by a snake. I hobbled screaming to mother, terrified and in pain, the sole of my little foot frighteningly red and visibly swelling. I threw myself impetuously into her arms as she sat embroidering on the terrace. With considerable presence of mind, she cut my foot with her small scissors and lifted it to her mouth and sucked out the venom. I remember the doctor who was called in saying to Mother, "You saved his life, but you were lucky you had no cuts in your mouth."

I let slip then, unwisely, of course, the information about my lost position, though, out of pride, I maintained I had voluntarily given up the work rather than being obliged to depart in disgrace.

Mother smiled up at me obviously pleased. She had sufficient tact, however, not to remind me that she had said, when I first took the position, "Why on earth would you want to do work of that kind?" I'm not sure what kind of work she had in mind for me, if any. Mother has spent her life avoiding work. "Perhaps you will consider giving up that awful, dark flat and moving back here, at least until you decide what you are going to do?" she asked me, tilting her head toward me, as we entered the hall.

I stood blinking in the muted light and said, "Perhaps," listening to Mother's panting and feeling her slight weight on my arm. I had recently had an idea for an historical novel. Might my work consist in staying home and writing and taking care of Mother as so many devoted sons had done? Besides, it would be difficult to earn a living, after what had happened, and where else would I go? I said, "In any case I'm going to try and come over more often."

Not one to let an advantage pass, Mother said, turning her head slightly to one side, lifting her fine eyebrows, "You would always be more than welcome here on a permanent basis."

As she said this, the hall, instead of growing lighter, as my eyes adjusted to the gloom, had, on the contrary, grown darker, and I stumbled over the Persian carpet and knocked my knee against the kist.

"Go wash your hands, darling. Lunch will be ready soon. I want to have time for our talk. And there's the surprise!" Mother said coyly.

"Ah, the mystery person," I said looking around as if he or she might be lurking. Then, obediently, I went into the cloakroom with its basin and rain gear. I was staring at my pale, freckled face and pale eyes through the heavy glasses— my father's small eyes in the mirror—when someone knocked.

The new secretary offered me a clean hand towel. I thanked her, and as she remained stiffly in the doorway, I said, "You didn't tell me your name?" She shook her head. I turned toward the basin and washed my hands. "Bertha," she said softly.

I looked up at her reflection in the mirror. She observed me with her anxious eyes, biting on her under lip. I continued scrubbing furiously as though I, and not Jakob, had been digging in the earth, and she left the room.

When I emerged, I descended the steps into the lounge which leads into the dining room. As usual the velvet curtains were closed on the afternoon light. A fly buzzed against the windowpane, trying to escape. In the dim light, I drew myself up, thinking of the long luncheon ahead, looking at the delicate Louis XV furniture and light Pierneef paintings which Mother had collected over the years and which grace the long, narrow room. Mother, though she has never put it to good use, is a woman of considerable education, and much taste, though her greatest skill lies in manipulating those around her.

I should never have mentioned my lost position to Mother, I realized. I believe I may have smacked my forehead, or made some gesture of that sort, and I may even have muttered, "You idiot!"

Then I noticed the secretary in one corner, standing unobserved in the shadows by the drinks' tray, in her dark clothes. "Your mother told me to offer you a drink," Bertha said and considered me with her earnest, intelligent gaze, the thin, unsmiling lips. I wondered if she had seen me smack my forehead, and if I had really said the words aloud. Had she heard me muttering to myself?

I watched as she squeezed a piece of lime into the glass and stirred the ice with a swivel stick and handed the drink directly to me with only a linen napkin underneath. As I took it, her damp palm touched mine, accidentally, perhaps. She added with a half-smile, "You require anything else?" I was wondering if I detected a hint of hope, when Mother appeared at the top of the stairs and asked Bertha to pour her a whiskey and soda. "Of course," she said solemnly and hurried to fulfill Mother's wish.

When she had left the room, I asked Mother who she was. She had come with unusually good references, actually, could I imagine, had a degree in philosophy. Her parents had been killed recently in a car accident, poor darling, leaving nothing but debts. She came from a large English family of some distinction, Mother maintained. The poor young thing was trying to do what she could for them—innumerable brothers and sisters— Mother thought there might actually be six, who all adored her, and counted on her. She had needed a place to stay, and a position, cash for all the boarding schools—would do anything to help. Missed her family terribly.

I said nothing, thinking of the boy who had brought about my downfall—also an orphan and on a scholarship and ostracized by the other boys in his class, while Mother went on about Bertha, how bright, what a good head for figures she had, how resourceful, or perhaps how accommodating—I believe was the word she used. She maintained the girl could sew, cook, and was wonderful with small children.

Mother prattled on even as we sat down at table. "Despite her many qualifications, Bertha has accepted to help us with our finances," Mother smiled up at her as Bertha, herself, to my surprise entered and sat down quietly on Mother's left, followed by the maid who brought in the silver tureen with the steaming potato soup which she placed on the sideboard. I realized then what the good odor had been, as Bertha rose and offered the tureen to Mother.

Bertha stood on Mother's left so that we were facing one another with Mother between us at one end of the dining room table, the French doors open on the garden, but the curtains closed, so that, as Mother would say, every servant in the garden could not stand and gape at each mouthful she ate. As the breeze lifted the curtain, however, I caught a glimpse of Jakob's back as he crouched, bent over from his great height, picking flowers. He already held a large bunch of mauve and yellow blooms cradled in his arm and as the breeze blew the curtains up in the air, like a sail filling with wind, Jakob stood erect and swiveled to face me, as though he had sensed my regard on his slender back. For a moment, our gaze met above the flowers he held, just as Mother pressed her stockinged foot against my leg and arched her eyebrows at me to indicate Bertha's presence and get my attention. "Bertha is simply wonderful with figures, and has umpteen degrees," Mother said.

I said, "I'm sure she does," thinking of the headmaster who had called me into his paneled study and said, "Despite all your degrees, you understand how difficult it is for me to recommend you, now."

"Serve Peter first, it's his favorite soup," Mother said impatiently.

"No, no," I protested and insisted Mother serve herself, so that Bertha moved with the tureen toward me and then toward Mother, swinging her hips back and forth, as though in some rhythmic dance. When, finally, conforming to mother's wishes, she passed me the bowl, I was almost certain she deliberately brushed her knee against mine.

After luncheon Mother insisted on our retiring *en tête-à-tête* to her study. She said, "Now you will have time on your hands, darling, you will be able to take an interest in our business."

I sat down opposite her at her desk and tilted back my chair and smothered a yawn. I had eaten and drunk more than I should have and was overcome with drowsiness. What I wanted was to lie down and sleep somewhere undisturbed.

"And don't swing on that chair, it's a precious one," Mother added.

"Oh, Mother," I protested, but she was rubbing at her glasses to clear them, bringing out heavy, serious-looking files from her desk drawer and paging through them.

"Now just take a look at this," she was saying when someone scratched on the door.

"Our mystery guest?" I asked hopefully, thinking that even some dull friend of mother's would be preferable to this. But it was just Bertha with the coffee.

Mother ignored her, while she poured from both silver pots, one with a white handle, the other with a black one to indicate the milk and the coffee, pouring with dexterity into the delicate gold-rimmed demitasses. Mother said: "I want you to realize just how much there is to manage. A rich man, you must know, one who should at this point be thinking of settling down," she said softly, her face flushed from the wine and the food, and perhaps the contemplation of her wealth. The light was on her face as she lifted it towards me, and I couldn't help thinking how young and amazingly lovely she still was.

I coughed and jerked my head toward Bertha who went on pouring the hot liquids into the cups, her thin lips twitching anxiously. But Mother responded, "Bertha knows all, don't you, Bertha, darling? There must be at least..." she was saying, running her finger down a list of figures, as Bertha handed me my cup. In some prearranged scheme, or her confusion, or my embarrassment, between the two of us we dropped the cup, splashing hot coffee all down my trousers and thigh.

"Oh, for goodness sake!" Mother exclaimed and rose, too, to help, dabbing at me with her handkerchief while Bertha stood back and eyed me with her wild hare's eyes.

"Well, don't just stand there, Bertha!" Mother exclaimed. "Help him!"

Bertha picked up the cup from the carpet.

"Take your trousers off and put ice on your leg," Mother ordered. I stared. Did she expect me to disrobe in the middle of her study, with the secretary there!

"Go upstairs and take off your trousers. Get ice for him, Bertha," Mother said.

Bertha and I left the room together in silence, and I walked up the stairs to the spare room which led off the landing. I closed the door behind me. I was sweating, and my thigh was burning. I stood in the middle of the room which had once been mine. Nothing was changed: the four-poster bed, with its blue checked bedcover, where Mother would come to kiss me good night, sitting beside me for a moment, her perfume lingering when she left; the model boat I had made for her on the dresser; the old armoire with the mirror on the door. The sun was on the smooth green lawn, the heavy quiet of the October afternoon. Somewhere in the distance a bird called out three times: high, high, low. I wanted to simply lie down and sleep.

I removed my trousers, wet a flannel with cold water in the bathroom, and pressed it against my burning thigh and closed my eyes.

When I came back into the bedroom in only my shirt and underpants, the burn turning purple on my thigh, Bertha was standing at the door with a blue and white striped bowl of ice in her hands. She watched me come into the room and said, "Sit on the bed, please," and came over to me. I sat down, but said, "I can do that, myself," and reached for the bowl, but she shook her head and held onto it as if her life depended on it.

She took a piece of ice and bent over me and pressed it against my thigh. She rubbed the ice slowly and soothingly round and round, letting it melt against my hot leg, the liquid dripping down between my thighs. Then she slid down with a supple noiseless movement onto her knees before me. She put the bowl down and bent over my dripping thigh, her fair hair falling forward and covering her face. She pressed her thin lips like a balm against my burn. She licked my wound, her tongue traveling up my leg to the edge of my underpants. She slipped the cotton to the side and pressed her lips tentatively against my sex. Then she opened her mouth and sucked like a small child.

I thought of the disastrous display of misplaced affection for the orphan boy whose solitude had so moved me that, in a moment of passion, I had been foolish enough to write an inappropriate letter which had been treacherously turned in to the headmaster by the object of my desire. I shut my eyes, put my head back, let myself go and forgot my pain as I heard myself whisper his forbidden name.

When I opened my eyes, Bertha was still on her knees looking up at me. She crossed her hands, pulled her shirt over her head with one swift movement, letting her heavy white bosoms swing free. The breasts seemed to me in some strange way not to belong to the narrow body, the small waist, the pink, childlike face.

I sat there for a moment, my legs apart, staring down into her green eyes which were now so close to me that I was able to see not only their brown flecks but the desperation and deep sadness there. I smelled again that strong odor of panic, and thought of her dead parents, her little brothers and sisters, her years of study of a difficult discipline which had brought her to this moment, on her knees, her head like a dog's between a stranger's legs. She put her hand to her small mouth, and I was afraid she might gag.

"The first time you have ever done that," I said and put my hand on her shoulder.

She said nothing, just staring at me, hope in her eyes.

"I'm so very sorry about your parents—your family, your—" I hesitated. Then, for some reason, I remembered the servant Jakob, who must be waiting for me to claim the flowers he had picked. I imagined him standing in the middle of the lawn with a huge bouquet of light flowers in his dark arms.

I sang out, "But I just can't!" and sprang up fast, pulled on my trousers and ran down the stairs and out the front door.

The silver-blue Lancia was still there in the sunshine. This time as I rushed past it, going to my own old Morris, I noticed a piece of paper propped up on the windscreen. I went nearer to the car, leaned on the hot metal, and read the words, "Happy Birthday, Peter, love Mother," written in red.

The keys to the car dangled from the ignition. On a sudden impulse, I jumped into the black leather seat and reversed fast over the gravel. I was turning the car around when I saw Jakob come running wildly across the driveway in his khaki shorts, waving a big bunch of purple and gold flowers. He shouted, "Your flowers! Don't forget your flowers!"

"Jump in," I shouted back and threw open the door, and we gunned it down the driveway and all the way out of the iron gates.

Youth

The light was blinding. I was giddy with the brightness, the height, the magnitude of the mountains. You walked ahead of me without looking back, oblivious of the wild flowers at your feet: columbines, bluebells, and white irises like candles, scintillant in the early morning light. White with foam, churning, the water resounded down the gorge, so loud I could hardly hear you speak. Without stopping to look back, you shouted, "We are almost at the top."

But we were not. You climbed steadily, with long strides, springing forward silently in your dusty, thick-soled boots. Your ivory calves gleamed, as slender and smooth as a girl's. You had tied your shirt around your narrow hips, and your broad back was bare, your silky shoulders exposed. Your pale hair melted in the sunlit air that quivered about your head.

My head was spinning, my mouth dry. The path flattened out for a while, and I caught my breath, looking down into the valley with its smooth green fields, and below that the orderly village, all washed by the same clear mountain light, all clean, fresh, and harmonious.

You waited in a pool of shade and looked back at me. I was struck by the mysterious contrasts in your face: your eyes a lush violet, the lashes long and black, the skin smooth and pale except for the bold, purple bruise beneath your chin which you carried like a blazon, the insignia of your profession. You took my hand and helped me over the roots of a tree.

Big boulders shaded the mountain's summit. No flowers grew there, no water ran, and even the skeletal pine trees clung precariously to thin soil. There was no sound, no bird song, not even the buzzing of a fly.

Only the light was the same: dazzling.

You sat in the shade, the earth slippery and scented with pine. I leaned back against your chest, and drank from the cool water you poured into my open hands. I splashed it on my hot face, my neck.

You said, "Look," and stretched out your arm, and the shadow fell like a dark wing. All the world spread before me: the maroon mountains, the green valley, the sparkling river, the vast azure sky. All of this had existed for centuries, the sea had receded, the mountains surged forth, the flowers had blossomed, so that this instant could occur for me. The view was endless, the possibilities infinite. I left myself behind, escaped my suffering flesh. I plunged and plummeted. I was the water shining below us, the white aspen bark. I was the light on your face. As you held me in your arms and told me that we could meet that evening, I was winged, perched, free to fly.

You never said when we would meet, but almost every day you summoned me. I hovered by the telephone in the dark hall as though it were a volcano about to explode. At any hour, I would slip out of the narrow house my parents rented for the summer and bicycle up the path through the trees recklessly. I was always bicycling, the sun coming and going in my eyes, alternately plunged into shadow and blinded by the glare, going on breathlessly along the path that led into the village and the hotel where you stayed. I feared nothing, not my father's wrath, my mother's concern, nor the musicians' gossip, not even your wife. You had told me your wife was not coming up there until the end of the music festival. You never spoke of love. You did not speak much, but now and then your face would turn bright, your lovely eyes grow opaque, as though curtained by a film, and you would look into the distance and talk of music, the voice of the violin. I remember your hands, the fingers blunt-tipped, strong: peasant's hands.

On the morning we climbed to the summit, you told me you had to go to a rehearsal. "What a bore. I have to rehearse with Kyata," you said shrugging your shoulders. Do you remember the child prodigy, a few years younger than I, the plump Korean girl, with flat, shiny cheeks who played the piano so magnificently? You were going to play Brahms, I recall, a sonata for violin and piano. I asked to accompany you. You said it was time to go, you had to change your clothes.

In your hotel room the Venetian blinds were shut. I could hear the river rushing beneath your window and a mourning dove calling. You opened the slats and the sunlight lay like a golden ladder on your bed.

I stood at your dresser staring at the old misty photo of your home. I still remember the name of the village in Southern Germany where you lived. You said a factory near there made the famous aspirin.

The photo was taken on a gray day, or the photographer had deliberately created an impression of mystery. The turreted house was dimly seen through the iron grill of the gate. Weeping willows lined the driveway. A small pale girl stood at the end of the white path in a dirndl. I suppose she must have been your daughter although you never mentioned her.

I examined your collection of rocks. I was admiring a luminous pink rock with concentric blue lines, when you came and stood beside me. You said it was I who was beautiful, and we smiled at one another in the mirror. I was dazzled by the glow in my eyes. I climbed avidly into your bed.

You walked through the streets blindly in the glare of light, without looking right or left. Musicians were the gods in that town: you expected the cars to wait for you, and they did. People recognized you in the street. On one side, smooth green lawns stretched, and on the other elegant shops opened their doors. We walked past the marble garden. You walked fast with long strides, in silence, already concentrating on your music.

We were late. You asked the boy with the programs at the entrance of the tent if Kyata were waiting for you. "The whole world is waiting for you," the boy said, smiling at me, with complicity. He had a pleasant voice, a friendly freckled face. He wore very short shorts and a daisy in his buttonhole.

The vast tent was filled except for a few seats up front reserved for you and your guests. Yellow light filtered through the giant canvas. Faded flowers from the night before, gladioli and chrysanthemums, wilted at the edge of the stage. Kyata wore a salmon-pink dress with a full skirt which made her look plumper than ever and ridiculous. I wondered who had advised the dress. Her flat baby face shone with sweat. She sat at the piano nervously wiping her hands on her full skirt. She half-stood awkwardly when you climbed quickly up the steps to the stage. Her face was fulvous as you bowed ceremoniously over her hand. She made a false start, immediately became flustered, apologized profusely. The conductor said something kind about first performances, and she recommenced. Then I forgot everything except the music.

I opened my eyes when I realized the man beside me was giggling. A dog had wandered down one of the aisles and was sitting as though listening almost at your feet. Kyata kept glancing nervously at the dog and then at you from the corner of her small eyes, her little plump fingers moving up and down the keys all the while with amazing expertise. The wind picked up and blew over some chairs with a clatter. Orange paper wrappers floated through the air like confetti. Everyone laughed. Kyata kept playing valiantly, and looking up at you. For a moment I thought she would burst into tears. You played the way you made love, with your whole body. You bowed, your hair falling forward over your eyes. The applause was rapturous.

We climbed the road back to your hotel. You took my arm and squeezed it tightly against your ribs. You glanced at me tenderly. You seemed very happy. We sat down in the marble garden, and you tilted your chin toward the sun. Your face looked the way flowers do sometimes, lit from within. The boy who had greeted us at the tent walked by with the daisy in his buttonhole and waved at us. You muttered, "Another aspiring violinist. There are altogether too many up here."

I wanted to talk about music, Kyata, to ask you if someone so young could express the emotion inherent in great music. "When I was fifteen," I began.

You said you had forgotten the Brahms score. "What an idiot," you said, slapping your brow. I offered to go back for it. You said, "Run along and meet me at the hotel," as though I were a child.

In the tent I found Kyata sitting alone at the piano, her head bowed, her soft shoulders slumped, her hands on the keys. She lifted her head when she saw me, wiped her puffy, red eyes. Sweat stained her satin dress.

"He forgot his score," I told her. She rose and helped me look for it. She trumpeted into a gray handkerchief and gushed, "He's so wonderful, amazing. Only the Germans are that good. No one else plays with such precision, such controlled emotion. He's so dedicated to his work, so disciplined. He has such faultless technique, so..." she began to sob.

I wanted to give her a hug, even to kiss her plump cheek. Instead I told her what my mother told me when she saw me weeping over you. I said, "You should get out into the sunshine." She wiped her puffy eyes with the handkerchief and nodded miserably. "Maybe I'll walk around awhile," she mumbled.

I should have told her how well she had played, how young she was, or said something about not wasting a beautiful day on the sorrows of love.

She said, "I'll be all right, don't worry."

I looked at the gladioli, the paper wrappers on the floor, a fly buzzing around her head. "I have to run," I said, clutching your score to my breast.

I ran along the street. The sun seemed even brighter, the lines clearer. The street looked cleaner than ever. I noticed the people surging down the street like a bright shining river.

How happy they looked, all strolling in the sunshine, packages in hand, dressed in all the colors of the rainbow; they were tanned, healthy, young! Even the well-brushed dogs shone, frisking unleashed down the street. In the shop windows, jewelry glittered, cloth shimmered, a straw hat with a bright red rose caught my eye. I smelled the fresh bread from a bakery. My reflection gleamed for a moment in a shop window: my legs long and smooth and tanned, my white shorts crisp, my pink and white striped shirt as smooth as ice cream; my eyes glowed radiantly. And when I looked up, the clouds above me were pure white and seemed close enough to pluck, like white chrysanthemums from the sky. Everything seemed bathed by Kyata's unhappiness, washed by her tears.

You were waiting for me in the cavernous lobby of the Victorian hotel. You came toward me immediately as I emerged from the revolving door. You clasped my hands and whispered that something had happened. Your wife was arriving that night. I remember the concierge behind the polished wooden desk, the heavy key in his hand, the maroon velvet chairs, the beam of sunlight penetrating the heavy curtains, motes of dust. The sunlight slid from your arm as you put it around my shoulders, to steady me. You murmured, "It's all right. It makes no difference, darling..." and ushered me into the elevator. As it climbed you said you could not leave me, you were going to tell your wife. She would give you a divorce. Then we would be together, able to...

For a long moment I looked directly into your violet eyes. They were limpid, as though a film had dropped from them. I could see straight through them, through your high white forehead. I could see what you were thinking. I remembered you telling me what an expert housewife your wife was, how she washed and ironed, packed for you, put up jam. I wondered if you were going to ask me to pack your suitcase, to gather berries. I had never ironed a shirt in my life. The elevator went on climbing and climbing, slowly in silence.

I said nothing. What could I tell you? Could I say that I had realized in that instant that I did not love you, that I did not love anyone as yet, that what I loved was life? Could I say that I wanted to live alone, to see the world through my own eyes?

"We will be together, won't we?" you asked leaning toward me. I drew back.

It was very cool and dead quiet in the long carpeted corridor. There was a bowl of artificial flowers on a polished table. I said, "Here's your score. You know when I fetched it, Kyata was weeping. She seemed very upset."

You said, "Thank you. You better go now," but I stood in the corridor and watched your tense back, as you struggled miserably and ineffectually with the key in the dim light.

I wandered idly into the marble garden and sat down on one of the white stones, the sun lingering sweetly on my legs. The shadows fell obliquely across the grass. I watched as an enormous orange sun dipped behind the blue mountains. The light was amber. I saw Kyata walk by in the distance, her plump shoulders stooped, her head bowed. She waved enthusiastically, and I waved back. I shut my eyes. I was almost asleep, when I felt someone's shadow fall on me. For a moment I thought it was you. I imagined you had followed me, come to recriminate, to beg, but it was not you. Do you remember the music student?—the one who had told us everyone was waiting. No one knew his name back then. He still had the daisy in his buttonhole. His wide smile lit up his freckled face.

Poor Cousins

For my maiden great aunts: Maud, May and Winnifred.

"Here he is," we all whispered, as we spied the young man who strode so unsuspectingly, so enthusiastically along the dust road to our house in the heat of the December afternoon.

This was Kimberley, early in the twentieth century, when men still flocked to the diamond town and stood on the edge of the Big Hole and contemplated the number of people swarming down the sides with their picks, shovelling the loose blue soil, and dreamed of riches. It was the time when the water cart would wake us in our small, hot bedrooms in the mornings, as it sprinkled water on the roads in an effort to settle the invincible dust, and when we were still greatly troubled by swarms of flies.

We were sitting out on the narrow verandah, where we spent most of our days, in an effort to escape the trapped heat of our small house with its corrugated iron roof and thin, plastered walls. Despite the heat and dust and flies our mother did not tolerate idleness in her girls. She insisted we rise early and take up our work before nine. We crocheted blankets; we embroidered tablecloths, table napkins, initials on sheets; we made beaded handbags; we knitted, we did petit point or we darned our clothes, and we gossiped—how we gossiped!—endlessly and often about our cousins, who lived not far from us but in a better part of town. We spoke of their fine clothes, their diamonds, and the receptions they gave in their grand home, to which we were not often invited, or, if we were, received the invitation ignominiously at the last minute.

Only after luncheon, in the high heat of the afternoon, were we finally allowed to retreat to our beds and our books. "No reading in the mornings!" Mother would say severely, as though it were a great sin. Sammie, our youngest or *laatlam* (late lamb), born when mother was already fifty years old, was particularly fond of reading novels. She read George Eliot and Jane Austen and the Brontë sisters, who were, like us, three girls. Sometimes she would sneak into the bathroom to finish a chapter or two on the sly in the morning.

On this December afternoon Sammie watched, as we all did, as the young man climbed our steps two at a time in his shiny new boots, his waist coat and fob watch. He sweated in the heat and dabbed at his forehead with a fine white handkerchief. Mother rose to welcome him and to shake his hand with some enthusiasm. He looked at her with pleasure, too, we suspected. Mother, at sixty-seven, was still, though heavy, a handsome woman, in her good pink silk dress with the ruffles around the neck, a frizz of white curls on her forehead.

She introduced us all to him, as she had done to so many before. "My three daughters," she said, smiling at him: "Crawford, Brett, and Sam," running our names together as though we were one.

He looked us over, his dark brown gaze lingering on each of our faces in turn, as we lifted them toward him.

We are three girls in our family, as are our cousins, our mother's brother's children, who are about the same ages as us. They are Maud, May, and Winnifred, but we have been given boys' names for some reason, perhaps because of our lost brothers.

At twenty-five Crawford was still slender and shy, with gentle blue eyes and wispy blond curls, which she washed with lemons to heighten the blond lights, and fluffed up around her face with her fine, white fingers, which always trembled a little as she worked or when she helped us button our dresses. At twenty-three Brett was taller and plumper and bolder with pink cheeks and deep brown eyes—perhaps the prettiest of us all, with her freckled skin and rebellious brown curls which she washed in beer to bring out the red lights and tied back from her face with a black velvet ribbon. Sammie was only seventeen, that December day. She had always been fragile and somewhat wayward, as a result of being cosseted and Mother's pet. She had light green eyes with a sort of distant, hazy expression, which made them seem almost transparent. She still got to bathe in milk to keep her skin so delicately pale, and her hair was a pale wheat color, too. The two dead boys were Eugene, whom none of us remembered, as he was born first and only lived to be three and drowned in the river behind the house. There was a baby boy, too, who died at birth, as so many infants did in those days.

Now, Mother gestured graciously to this young man to sit in the wicker chair. She asked him if he would care for a cup of tea, on this hot day, or perhaps he might want to indulge in something stronger? He nodded his blond head and flashed his teeth with some enthusiasm and wiped his brow and said he would start with tea and might go onto something stronger, surveying our cramped verandah, the wicker furniture which Sammie's cat had scratched, and the thin maidenhair fern which drooped in a pot, and the three of us sweating in our best silk dresses. Mother sent us off to bring out the tea tray, which we had prepared earlier in the kitchen.

We left the verandah, but not before we had got a good look at the chap, or should we risk using the phrase *the fly*, we were hoping to catch in our web?

He sported a mustache which drooped at the sides, and gave him a slightly mournful and interesting air. His soft dark eyes, taking in the scene, seemed innocent or if not innocent, unaware. He had an embarrassment of riches in his large white teeth, which he was willing to share with us, flashing them at us generously. He brushed his blond forelock back to show us his low forehead. We all decided he was one of the most promising of the many candidates we had seen.

Mother had already shown us a picture of the man several days before. We had studied his portrait carefully. We scrutinized at our leisure the strong broad shoulders and what appeared to be sturdy legs in the high boots and the large hands on the hips. From a good English family, Mother had said and cocked her head to one side approvingly. He had recently sold a farm in Natal. We had heard about the blue banana trees on the farm and the dogs. He had brought several dogs with him, apparently. Sammie, who loved animals, approved of this and reminded us that our cousins loved dogs, too.

"Attractive, don't you think?" Mother had said, taking the picture carefully from us and asking for our opinion on the matter. We had all agreed. "And quite prosperous, I gather. He's here in Kimberley for the diamonds, apparently, like so many of them. Perhaps a little on the extravagant side, has already acquired a few debts on the gaming table, drunk a little too much champagne in the company of women, but what young man who comes to this town does not behave in this way?"

Crawford murmured something understanding. Crawford was always very understanding. Sammie, in her innocence, said she thought he looked like a good man. Brett said he didn't look too bright to her, but he would do just fine for our purposes. Mother put his photograph into an envelope with all the others and placed it behind the clock on the mantelpiece.

Mother had an unfailing ability to track down these young men, who came to our town and had a certain unsuspecting swagger about them. They strode down our road and climbed our steps two at a time, not knowing what lay ahead. She sniffed them out, ferreted them from their hiding places and brought them forth for her inspection and ours. She read the newspapers, the gossip columns, the ladies' magazines, and any periodicals which spoke of single men of some stature and social position who might have a small flaw or two. They were not difficult to find, as there were still many more men around here than women, so many of them having come to the diamond fields to make their fortunes.

Mother was particularly tolerant where these men were concerned. She looked for them anywhere she could find them. She kept up with old friends and acquaintances, sometimes even wrote to strangers, making up some story of having known a relative of theirs. "A little white lie in a good cause," she would tell us, as she lay down her pen and passed around her letter, as we sat around her on the verandah. We would read her adroit words, which seemed to say something but did not actually say anything at all. We would smile and go on with our handiwork.

We had been up early that morning, because we knew the suitor was coming, and each time one of them came, we could not help hoping, though so far we had not been successful in our endeavor.

We had helped the servant straighten up the house, and we had made our own beds and cut flowers from the garden for the vases. We had baked the scones ourselves and brought forth the good English raspberry jam. We had covered over everything with netting to keep off the flies, and we had spiked the pitcher of lemonade with something stronger, which was usually used for medicinal purposes, in order to produce a moment of euphoria in our victim and predispose him to our plan.

Now we crowded down the dark corridor of the house to fetch the tea tray to offer to this one, giggling a little at our game, but at the same time feeling too old for this sort of behaviour. We did not consider what we were doing sinful. As mother would say, "All is fair in love and war," and though this did not qualify exactly as either, we did not disagree. Even Sam, who sometimes voiced certain qualms of conscience, confessed to feeling that this time, we must be more persuasive. We must prevail. "He seems absolutely perfect, don't you think? How could anyone resist?" she whispered enthusiastically, while Brett put on the kettle, and Crawford measured out the tea carefully. We all nodded eagerly.

We often sent our only servant, a young maid, home on these occasions, to save money, but also because we felt she might simply hinder our maneuvers. As the years went by, this was becoming more and more serious work, we were aware. Time was running out for us.

We followed one another in solemn procession: Crawford, in her fine cream silk which she had inherited from one of our cousins, carried the tea pot; Brett, in the scarlet lace which had come from the same source, handled the tea tray; and Sammie, in pale mauve chiffon with leg-of-mutton sleeves and the décolleté which had once been Crawford's and was a little too tight for Sam and gave her the appearance of having more of a womanly figure than she actually possessed, brought up the rear with the spiked lemonade. In silence we trooped down the dark corridor and back onto the verandah.

Unlike our cousins' house ours is small and dark and very hot in the summer and cold in winter because of the corrugated iron roof. It has what is known as a shotgun corridor, which leads from the front door to the back, all the rooms leading off it on either side. We were all born here, and we had always lived here, and by this point we expected we would all go on living here all our lives, though that was not to be. We had lived here through the siege during the Boer War, when we had had to hide down in the tunnels built for our protection. It was Crawford who saw the native girl who was walking down the street, balancing a big bundle of washing on her head, the way they did, walking tall and straight, when the shell sent the head with the washing flying through the air. In this town where substantial sums of money were made and lost fast by whites and blacks alike, where black men had come to buy guns for their chiefs, and where the soil had been turned over constantly in the hope of spotting a diamond, we had all seen acts of violence at first hand.

The back garden is what we love the best about our house. It is quite large with a wild tangle of trees and long grasses, which lead down to the river. In those days, however, we spent much of our time in the shadows of the verandah. We swatted at the flies with a fly-catcher and kept our eyes peeled for the suitors, who were, our mother had explained, our only hope of salvation.

Though our family, according to Mother, on her side is descended from distinguished people, aristocrats, with a family crest—we are connected in some way with a Baron von Oudtshoorn and various distinguished judges—apparently, the Baron had been robbed of his lands, and our inheritance lost. Mother's older brother, our Uncle Charles, was a wealthy man, who had come to Kimberley about the same time as Cecil Rhodes. He had made his fortune in the diamond fields, but our poor mother had married our father, a dashing man with ginger sideburns, for love. He held a distinguished position as Government Secretary until after the death of his second boy, who was born just before Sam, when our father was involved in some kind of administrative scandal—we thought this was most unfair and were certain he had been unjustly accused—and was dismissed for "gross irregularities in keeping of the public accounts." He was brought to trial and actually sent to jail or rather, had had to spend six months in a hotel room, as the jail in the city was not considered fit to incarcerate a white man. We have never been told exactly where our father went after that, whether he took to the bottle or took his own life or took up with some other woman to overcome his shame. Mother never mentioned his name in our house and so we believed he came to some bad end.

Our Uncle Charles, our cousins' father, unlike our own, was devoted to his three girls and, indeed, quite fond of us, too. He had helped Mother in times of trouble with our school fees and had often paid Sammie's doctor bills. Unlike our missing father he spent a great deal of his time in his girls' company and watched over them most jealously.

As for us, we were, Mother had told us repeatedly, left entirely to our own devices. Our finances were in an increasingly precarious state. There was no respectable work which we were qualified to do, neither nursing nor teaching, which were about the only things a woman could do at that time, and Mother's family pride kept us from entering the trade: selling shoes or handkerchieves at the stores. She had another scheme in mind for our future.

When the three of us had returned to the attack on the verandah, Crawford helped Mother pass around the teacups, and Brett passed the buttered scones, and Sammie just sat back down on the swing-seat and sighed. She swung back and forth slowly, balancing her cup and staring at the suitor hopefully in the heat. We all stared at him. He asked if he might take off his jacket, and Mother said, "Please, please, go right ahead," and he stood up to perform this operation and we were able to admire his muscles through his fine shirt. We thought he looked increasingly attractive when he was in his shirt sleeves and silk waistcoat, sitting next to Sammie and talking openly about his ridgebacks and his farm, his mustache drooping in a melancholy way, swinging back and forth in the heat and the flies and what he must have realized, surely, were our straightened financial circumstances.

Crawford sat down in the wicker chair and blinked her big blue eyes, which filled so easily with tears, and took up her embroidery, which she had layed aside. Crawford is wonderful at embroidery. Brett stared at the suitor frankly with her dark brown eyes, and even young Sam at seventeen was taking a keen interest in the situation. She asked what were the names of his dogs, and he said there were three, and they were called Prince, Roger, and Savoy. The young man turned increasingly red under all this intense feminine scrutiny.

When the man asked for a glass of our special lemonade, Mother filled it to the brim and watched him gulp down the strong stuff. Then she brought up the subject quite directly, which we felt, because of the desperate circumstances, was wise. She turned to him, a little pink in the face, fanning her face with her heart-shaped fan, which our uncle had given her, and said, "You must meet my nieces, you know. They live on Inglewood Road, number fourteen, not far from here," and waved her hand airily in that elegant direction at the end of our street.

"Your nieces?" the man said, looking a little confused and staring at us, as though he thought he might have been mistaken in our identity.

We all nodded back at him, and Brett said brightly, "Our cousins: Maud, May, and Winnie, three girls just like us."

Our mother gushed on. "Such lovely girls they are, too, and such a lovely, big house. Their father, my brother, Charles, was very lucky on the diamond fields, you see, and was able to buy a handsome property for his family. He adores his three girls," Mother said with much enthusiasm, and smiled. Mother was not lying. Indeed our cousins were pretty girls, and indeed their house was fine, and their father did adore his girls. In fact, Mother always said that he could not bear the thought of parting with even one of his daughters, and his greatest fear was that they might marry someone unsuitable and leave him, alone. Our uncle, having lived in Kimberley for many years and having seen men do extraordinary things in order to acquire a fortune (one man had swallowed twenty-two diamonds in order to steal them), had become very suspicious as to men's motives and was convinced everyone was after his large fortune and the fine diamonds he had bestowed upon his three girls.

We all smiled and felt almost generous, at that moment, sharing this good news with the young man. After all, we could also have added that our Uncle Charles was ailing, that he had recently suffered a stroke, but did not, out of modesty. The suitor, too, looked rather pleased, though whether it was at this new prospect or not, we were not quite sure as yet. He kept on swinging on the swing-seat, looking almost dreamy, we thought. He seemed moved to write something down on a piece of paper, which we presumed was our cousins' elegant address. Perhaps it was just the spiked lemonade, provided for that reason, that had given his brown eyes a velvet softness, almost a look of sadness, and caused him to dangle one arm with abandon over the back of the swing-seat. Or was it, we wondered, the thought of these other girls, our cousins, after all, and so wealthy, with their diamond fortune, that brought the glow to his eyes and cheeks.

Mother smiled at the suitor in a suggestive way and said, "I've always loved my nieces, so pretty and fortunate and despite all they have, quite unspoiled, do you know? Girls who know how to keep a home," and waved her hands around our small one, the cramped verandah with the straggly maidenhair fern and the chipped china on the tray, where the flies had now settled on what was left of the scones. She gestured towards our small front garden, with its dusty hollyhocks and faded geraniums strangled in dry soil, to convey by contrast her nieces' fortune. What she managed to convey, quite simply, was wealth, their wealth, not ours, of course, untold wealth, which we knew their father, our Uncle Charles, had left to us in his strange will, in case any one of his daughters were to marry. He was willing to render all three of his daughters destitute, such was his fear of a man marrying one of them for his money. All we needed was one wedding for his fortune to pass from them onto us, the poor cousins.

The suitor continued to look a little surprised and disconcerted by Mother's words, but clearly he was feeling cheerful and in an expansive mood and asked for more lemonade. Mother raised her eyebrows slightly at what she must have considered, after all, an unnecessary expenditure at this point. Still she had Crawford fill his glass and looked at her watch and said, "I'm sure they would be delighted if you visited." Mother went on rather breathlessly to describe some of the interesting features of their house, a rather good collection of Timlin paintings, she said. "Did he know the painter, William Timlin, such a brilliant man, with such an unusual imagination?" The suitor shook his head and rose then and glanced at the three of us, a little sheepishly.

The sun was setting by then, and the shadows lengthening, and there was a pleasant cool breeze on the terrace. The suitor seemed loathe to move on. "I know they are on the lookout for just such a handsome and clever young man as you seem to be," Mother added and smiled most graciously. We all nodded and shook the young man's hand, and we all hoped the suitor would slip a note into one of our hands, asking her to meet him later that night, that one of us would be invited to slip out of the house after dinner and to rush recklessly along the road, even though, then, this suitor would never marry one of our cousins, so that we might inherit their fortune, but, instead, one of us. We were listening, pleased with our performance, as the suitor turned to leave, and go down our steps, as Mother added, "I wouldn't mention your visit to us to my nieces. Simply say a well-meaning neighbor gave you their name."

All the Days of My Life

She had been meaning just to go for a walk, to find the bookstore her husband had recommended, when she stepped into the church. At first she did not notice what was going on there. A Protestant church—the sign outside said it had been built many times, having been destroyed by fire and various calamities, before the current edifice was erected at the beginning of the last century. She had seen the brownstone spire from her hotel room. She had heard its bells, too, chiming every quarter hour, and the full number of hours on the hour. Sometimes they woke her, but she liked the sound which reminded her of her life in a small town in France where she had lived some time ago with her first husband.

The church had always been closed, the doors firmly and surprisingly locked—should a church's doors not always be open, a haven in time of trouble, a refuge from loss?—when she had tried to open them, on weekdays, which was the only time she was up in that town.

But this time, when she tried it, one of the side doors of the church opened easily, and she walked inside. A few well-built, dark-haired men stood about near the door, as though waiting for something. They looked at her and smiled almost welcomingly, as though she were expected.

She walked a way down the long side aisle, making a bit of a show of gazing around the pseudo-Gothic church with its high, narrow, stained-glass windows, as though she needed to explain her presence. She was, indeed, taken aback by the size of the church and the quality of the windows, but she was also somewhat self-conscious, feeling the men's eyes on her, now, walking slowly down the aisle in the long, narrow navy blue coat she had bought in France, and her good black hat, with the dark fur around the brim. She wore the hat pulled down a little to one side in a way which flattered her face, she felt.

She had come up there from the city in her good clothes by train the night before to join her husband, the second one. As was customary at that station, she had had to share her taxi with several people. The man sitting next to her had asked her where she came from, and what she was doing up here. She had laughingly told her husband, as he helped her take off her coat in the hotel room, that someone had tried to pick her up, which might or might not have been the case. She had cut the stranger short, replying that she was up here visiting her husband for a few nights, and they had traveled on in silence. Also, it was rather dark in the taxi, she had told her husband, which was true.

But her husband, a psychiatrist she had been married to for many years, had gallantly professed he was certain the man had wanted to pick her up. He had put his hands on her shoulders and drawn her to him and kissed her affectionately. He was grateful she had come up there, she knew, taken the tedious train ride along the river, left her daily routine, all her students' papers, just to be with him for a few nights, something she had not done for a while.

Now she could hear the loud sound of her high heels on the stone floor as she walked down the aisle. Then she realized a service was being held at the main altar and considered joining the congregation. Brought up in the Protestant faith, she had wanted to go to church for a while, but had had other obligations. She wondered what service it could be, and when it had begun. Odd that a mid-morning service was being held on a weekday in a church usually shut up during the week.

She stopped and looked at the small group of people in dark clothes before the altar. A thin woman was reading aloud from a white piece of paper, but from that distance she couldn't hear the words. A minister stood to one side in white robes.

Then she saw the box, covered with a yellow cloth marked with a black cross.

She slipped into a pew and onto her knees and closed her eyes. She said a prayer quickly, mumbled the words which came to her: *God stay with me, and guard me this day and all the days of my life.* Then she rose and walked down the side-aisle fast. A young, strong man with luxuriant dark hair opened the door for her and smiled in a friendly way as she left the church—a pallbearer, perhaps?

She thought of her little boy who had said to her once—he must have been about four years old: "When you are in your box, will you remember me?"

She walked up the hill through streets that were empty and cold and bleak and seemed to her the ends of the earth. The sun was a white disk burning behind cloud, and a thin coating of snow, which had turned to ice, covered the ground. Though there were large government buildings filled, she presumed, with many people, doing important things, they seemed empty, or populated with invisible, silent ghosts. Sometimes, in the summer at lunchtime, more people walked around, but now, late February, there was no one, and she felt strangely alone and outside of civilization.

She stopped to search her large handbag, and then all her pockets, for the address of the bookstore her husband had written down. She must have forgotten it in the hotel room. She remembered the street had the name of a bird, but all the streets up here seemed to have the names of birds: Dove, Lark, Eagle, Swan. She couldn't remember if her husband had said to turn left or right on Dove, or was it, perhaps, Lark? She remembered or thought she remembered reading somewhere once that the lark was the bird who mated *on the wing*, which, she presumed, meant while flying.

She walked one way and then the next. There was no one to ask, which was how she usually found her way, and each time she saw someone she hurried toward him or her, but the person vanished inside some door before she could reach him, almost as though avoiding her. There were no stores, either, to enter and to inquire within, no policemen in the streets, no one, only the narrow houses of the old town and the cold wind.

She tried to imagine ringing one of the doorbells and asking for information, but she couldn't conceive of anyone living in these houses. Where would they buy the bread, the milk? Yet the houses looked well-tended, even elegant, turn-of-the-century houses. Where had all the inhabitants gone?

She considered returning to her hotel, but she had already walked a long way and was loathe to give up now. Finally, when she was about to go back down the hill, she came across a bookstore on a corner. At first she thought her husband must have been misinformed: it was boarded up and had been closed down. Then she saw the entrance and walked into the surprisingly bright and clean place.

The man behind the counter had a rather antique appearance—his thinning long hair held back in a ponytail, Trotsky glasses, a gold earring. He greeted her amiably, telling her that if she needed any help she had only to ask, but did not rise. She smiled, grateful for the chance to browse without anyone hovering. No one slept in a chair, no one drank coffee; no one paged through magazine stacks, no one was reading aloud, no one stood in line, which, after the sort of city bookshops she was used to, was a great relief.

She soon found her way around the stacks, floating down the long aisles, amazed and delighted that in this place, where there were no people or any other stores, there could be so many fine books: poetry galore—she found a book of Delmore Schwartz's poetry she had been hunting for years, history and fiction and even a lovely bound book of Baudelaire's poetry in a bilingual edition, and all arranged alphabetically so that she could easily find her favorites. Someone had lovingly collected these books.

She had the elated feeling now of stepping out of time and space into a heavenly region. She gathered up several volumes—none of the books seemed to have any prices, and she wondered how the man, who could not see her, could trust her not to slip several volumes into her large black handbag. Perhaps he wouldn't have minded if she had. She could hear him speaking at length and very courteously to someone who seemed to be asking about some obscure out-of-print book. His voice was soft, cultivated and rather, she thought, like a florist's or an undertaker's.

When she approached him with the books, he stood up behind the counter, excused himself to the telephone caller, saying rather importantly, as though it were a rare occurrence, that he had to tend to a customer. He put the telephone down, and took the books from her and his glasses caught the light. She noticed his tight fitting blue jeans, a pleasant light-colored shirt and his dark, almost feminine eyelashes, the small, delicate ears. She thought now that she had known someone who looked like him, in her youth, a man who had been in love with her, wanted to marry her in the sixties, a man with a ponytail and identical Trotsky glasses, who had even worn an earring, a brilliant student at the university, who had gone off to Africa into the bush, caught sleeping sickness, and died.

While he marked down the prices of the books, she voiced her amazement at finding such a store in so deserted a place. "What a wonderful collection you have!" she said with enthusiasm.

He didn't seem to think there was anything astonishing about it. He said, "People will find you, wherever you are, if you make available what they need."

"I suppose so," was all she could think to reply, though she was not sure he was right. Mostly the opposite happened in life, it seemed to her: people did not find one another or what they needed, but she smiled and asked him how much she owed. The pile of books came to very little, she felt, and wondered how the man lived.

She told him, as she handed him the bills, what difficulty she had had finding him. "So confusing, all these birds' names, and I have the worst sense of direction. I walked around in circles for ages." Then, feeling tired, recollecting her long and confused wheeling through these streets, she asked him if there was a place for lunch around here. She wanted to sit down, eat and drink something, before she faced the walk down the hill. She wanted to delay returning to her empty hotel room. Her busy husband would not be back before late, she knew, and it was not the sort of information she could have asked of him. He had suggested she help herself copiously to the buffet breakfast, which came with the price of the room, and slip a little fruit or bread into her handbag for lunch, which, though perfectly possible, of course, was not something she felt she could do.

The man said, "Just around the corner there's a small place where I often go. Nothing fancy, sandwiches, that sort of thing. Glass of wine. Would that do?" She nodded, said it would do very well.

He would show her the way, to make sure she didn't get lost again, he declared. "I don't think I will miss too many sales!" he added and laughed—she noticed slightly yellow teeth. He picked up his bunch of keys, his gray coat, and his beret from the stool beside him, before she could think of what to say.

She laughed, too, at his little joke, but for a moment wondered if the man might not be some kind of criminal, and this empty bookstore in this deserted place, just a front for money-laundering? Could he be a member of the Mafia? Did this town have a Mafia? And what if he were to lead her down some narrow alley and into a dark corridor to a violent death? But would a criminal have so many books by Delmore Schwartz? Besides, in his slightly threadbare coat, and the navy blue beret, he didn't look at all like a criminal. When he opened the door, she went back out into the cold street and followed him.

Now that they were in the street, there was some constraint. Like the man the night before, he, too, asked her where she

143

came from, and what she was doing up here. She had never lost her accent, even after so many years. She said she had come up from the city, was here for a few nights staying in a hotel near the bottom of the hill, and she waved her hand vaguely in that direction. Probably better not to give too precise an address.

"Near the church?" he asked. She nodded and found herself telling him, at some length, about her visit to the church—even, for some reason, about the men's thick hair, and about what was going on in there. He made no reply, just glancing at her, while she spoke, in a wary way. She was afraid she might have sounded a little crazy, speaking to a stranger in this way about death.

They kept on walking down empty streets with the names of birds. They seemed to have been walking for a long time now, and she was tired. She wondered why he had said the place was just around the corner and where he was taking her. Eventually, she said, "Perhaps you could just point out the restaurant from here? I don't want to take up any more of your time," eager to get away from him now, embarrassed by her unnecessary disclosure, his continued presence on this lengthy walk.

"It's not far now, and I might as well come in with you, at this point. I usually lunch there—that is if you don't mind?" he said hesitantly.

She wasn't sure what to reply, but she didn't believe he would take a lunch hour on a regular basis, surely the busiest time for a bookstore of that kind. She felt an odd sensation of power, one she recognized from adolescence, or certainly one from her early youth, before her first marriage, before her child, who had arrived soon after she had married. For some reason she felt as though life were again full of possibilities, surprises, as though anything might happen. This man, after all, who must be ten years younger than she, had shut up his shop, had walked all this way in the cold wind, and because of her, because he wanted to have lunch with her, a stranger.

She had never really had this feeling of power with her second husband: she had courted him, going when he summoned her to his office late at night, when his last patient had left, and sometimes, in her eagerness, arriving too early, and, afraid she might bump into a patient in the lobby, having to walk around the block in the snow, with a heavy basket of food on her arm, food she had carefully cooked for him, the sort of food she might have made for a child: soups, stews, apple compote, which she had found out afterwards he disliked. He had accepted her obsession, her eagerness, her love with a sort of gentle, amused tolerance, it seemed to her. He was a good man, always courteous, kind, who would do anything for her, she was sure, but somehow, when she looked into his dark eyes, from time to time, she realized that this man, her beloved husband, was far, far away from her, that there was some part of him so far in fact that she would never reach it. At the same time, she realized that this was probably what had attracted her to him in the first place, may even simply have been an act on his part, the act of a psychiatrist who understood what was necessary to seduce someone like her.

So she glanced at the man and said, attempting nonchalance, "If you like."

"Is this all right?" he asked, as they came to a small hotel, a decent, discreet building, some five or six stories high. He opened the door to what appeared to be a rather dark restaurant. The receptionist asked if they wanted smoking or nonsmoking, and she said, "Non."

The receptionist sang out, "The greenhouse, then," which seemed a grand name for a drafty-looking, narrow, enclosed verandah.

"Will it be warm enough?" she asked warily, looking at the small table with the pink tablecloth by the brick wall under the big window. He said, "It should be," and she took her coat off, put it on a chair with her packet of books. She kept her hat on, as though it could protect her in some way from the cold, from this man, from whatever might transpire. She sat down, and the man sat down opposite her. She asked him what he recommended, and he ordered lunch for them: a bottle of white wine, salads, sandwiches.

He asked if she had a family, children, a question she was often asked, of course, and one she had grown adept at sidestepping. She said she had been married twice, and then that she needed to go to the bathroom, which was true, and rose and left the room. She entered the stall with relief to sit and find herself alone. Then she took off her hat and stood before the mirror in the bathroom in her navy silk blouse with the mother-of-pearl buttons, her dark skirt. She applied lipstick, rubbing a little onto her pale cheeks. She fluffed up her short dark hair with her fingertips. She had her mother's good, thick hair, which curled softly around her face, her mother's small hands and feet.

She wondered what the bookseller saw when he looked at her face. Certainly not what she saw, or even, perhaps, what others saw: her colleagues, her friends, even her husband. Though she had moved away, left her first husband, her home in France, her story had followed her, leaking behind her like a snail's trail. People whispered, she was sure, wondered how she had managed to go on with her life. Sometimes, they even commended her on her ability to continue with what they called "courage," a most overused word, she felt. She had simply done what she had to do.

They passed her story on from mouth to mouth, for the little thrill of it, the excitement, the attention given to the teller of the tale. She could imagine them saying, "D'you know what happened to her?—just the worst thing in the world." She knew it gave her a certain mystery, a sort of dark glamour, like a full-length black cloak which she wore perpetually; she could see this from the way people looked at her, with a kind of curiosity in their eyes, from their attempts to avoid certain subjects, which kept recurring, as if magically. She knew it from the awkward pauses, the gentle embraces, the kindnesses which were so hard to bear.

And she, too, had kept her sorrow alive, though she never spoke of it, perhaps because she never spoke of it. She kept it buried close to her heart, concealed, but tended daily, spreading through her whole body, her existence. In her heart of hearts she knelt before her loss, as before an icon with a lamp burning. She kept the lamp well oiled.

But this man saw none of this, she supposed. On the contrary, he had probably seen a glimmer of hope in her slanting, brown eyes. He had seen, perhaps, her still youthful shape, her narrow ankles, the slim calves. And would he take the skillful smear of lipstick for a blush of promise rising from her neck into her cheeks? Or should she just leave it at that? Perhaps she should slip quietly out the door, through the lobby, and escape while she could. And, perhaps, had she not left her good coat there on the chair, her packet of books, had the man not rather extravagantly ordered a whole bottle of wine, she might have slipped out the door and left him to eat his turkey sandwich by himself and nothing would have happened.

But she went back, sat down opposite the bookseller, drank from the glass of wine he had poured her.

They ate salads and surprisingly delicious turkey sandwiches on white toast with lettuce and tomato and mayonnaise and drank the white wine which was a little too sweet, but she did not care. They talked about books, their work. She taught French literature at a university in the city, had done her thesis on the influence of certain American writers: Hemingway, Faulkner, among others, on Camus. She said the things she usually said: what a struggle it was to get her students to read the classics, how rewarding when she found one who did, how distanced she sometimes felt from them so that she had difficulty understanding what they said. But she tried to get them to share her passion.

He said he had once been a schoolteacher himself at a private boys' school in the city, loved the work, but left to write a novel, which he had never written of course, but now sold the novels of others instead. "Much more useful," she said and drank her wine. He had moved up here, several years ago, with his partner, a successful mystery writer, who had bought the bookstore for him, he said.

She did not ask him, as she had once done, in what business he and his partner were engaged. She said nothing, just pressed her fingers against the cold windowpane above the table, as if against the keys of a piano. He mentioned his partner's name, asked if she knew his work. She nodded, said, "Of course," though she never read mysteries.

They liked it up here, the man said. "Quieter, more space," he explained. They lived in a house in the suburbs—nothing fancy, but with a good-sized garden. His partner liked to garden, when he wasn't writing mysteries.

She just looked at him, and thought how ridiculous she had been. She thought of a line in a book she had read once about an older woman who still thought she was beautiful. This man must simply have been hungry—indeed he was eating his sandwich with gusto—or at the most wanted a little companionship, unless he had something more sinister in mind? Or, on the contrary, had he sensed her distress in the street, and felt she needed companionship? Was it possible he had simply wanted to be kind?

As if he guessed her thoughts, he said, "You are a very lovely woman, do you know?" and touched her hand lightly, looking at her over the rim of his glasses, slightly amused. She noticed the pale blue of his eyes, the dark eyelashes, the glint of gold in his small delicate ear, and thought again of the young man who had wanted to marry her. She remembered how he had walked her through the streets of Paris all one night, trying to convince her. What would have happened if she had consented? Would he have stayed in France, not gone off to Africa to catch some exotic disease? How different might her life have been? She supposed everyone had a story of this kind. She remembered her mother telling her of her marriage to a man before she was of age, which her parents had annulled. Was such a thing possible?

She said, "You don't have to say that."

He patted her hand in a kind way and asked her, "And what brought you here, to this country?"

She found herself, unaccountably, telling this stranger, what she never told anyone: how she had married young, had a child immediately, a little boy; how she had moved away, left the house in France, after her divorce, though it was very beautiful—an old mill, with a river that ran beneath it, silver willows along the bank. She spoke without looking at the man, without seeing him, directing her words to the window so that her breath misted the glass.

It was not in that house that the accident had occurred. She had been visiting friends in Paris, an old friend from the university, an Englishwoman who had married a Hungarian, Yonchi. She remembered his name, though she had never seen them again. They had two adorable little boys—lived in the Latin Quarter, a bohemian life. Her friend came from a wealthy English family—there were lovely pieces of furniture, but she had peeled the beans for lunch sitting on the floor in the living room, carried a cock around on her shoulder—that sort of thing.

It was a weekend in the summer—such an unusually hot, humid Parisian day, she said, trying to catch her breath, now, as though the drafty verandah with its large windows had suddenly lost all air.

It was no one's fault, of course. She didn't blame anyone, only herself. They were all so young. They had all had a lot of wine to drink with lunch, were sitting around the table, while the children were playing in the back bedrooms, which looked over the courtyard. She could hear their voices, squeals of laughter, footsteps running, but she had not gone back to see, though she remembered thinking she should. An apartment on the sixth floor. An open window. One of the little boys, not her little boy, had come running in, red in the face, to tell them. She found it difficult to breathe, but she looked at the stranger now, told him, "Like all little boys, I suppose, he wanted to fly."

She was weeping silently, and the man—she still didn't know his name—had abandoned his turkey sandwich, his wine, was leaning toward her—his face shiny, holding her hand in his hard grip. He was offering his gray handkerchief and mumbling something about a miracle being required for a child to grow up, unscathed. The tears continued to fall across her face onto her navy silk blouse, her breasts. She was heaving. People were looking at her, at them.

He paid the bill, picked up her coat, her packet of books, took her by the arm. They walked into the dark lobby of the hotel together. She thought just for an instant that people must take them for an old but still loving couple: she turning her face into his arm, he hovering over her protectively. He said, "One minute." Obediently, she waited, leaning against the dark red wall of the hotel lobby, looking down at the arabesque pattern in blues and red, while he conferred with someone, a small man with a bandage over one eye, who stood behind a counter.

He held her hand and led her into the small elevator, which kept ascending, several flights. She followed him along the corridor, head down, still weeping. But now she felt a sort of subtle lethargy and submission. She did not care where he was taking her, or what he intended to do to her there, and the room, when he had opened the door with the key, and they had entered, seemed quite satisfactory for whatever were to happen there: dimly lit, clean and respectable, though somewhat dingy with its dull red bedspread, a clock on the mantelpiece, heavy velvet curtains which sagged over the window, its tired air of private woes and sins, the lingering hint of smoke.

He said again, "Just a minute," and went through the door into the bathroom. She could hear the water running.

Automatically, she walked over to the window, pulled aside the curtain and struggled with the handle. She opened it, felt the cold air on her face with relief. She leaned out, looked down into the narrow street, and in her mind saw the small body lying there in the gray shorts, the striped shirt, the dusty bare feet. She thought of her prayer in the church. What had God done to protect her that day or any of the days of her life?

She thought of her husband who would wait for her that evening, of course, but would go on with his busy, useful, thoughtful life; she thought of the drama of such an act, the moment in the air, the flying.

Then he came to her quickly and shut the window behind her firmly, turned her to face him. He put his hand directly on her damp, silk blouse, lifted it away from her skin, where her tears had fallen, where it clung to her breasts. He unbuttoned her blouse, loosened it from her skirt, slipped his hands up her back and unfastened her bra. He lifted up her damp breast, leaned his head down, found her nipple with his mouth. She put her arm around his head, cradled it.

It was only when she had walked down the hill and entered the lobby of her hotel that she realized that she had forgotten her good black hat with the fur around the brim. Had she left it in the bathroom or on the chair, perhaps, in what the receptionist had called so grandly "the greenhouse?" Or was it upstairs on the carpet in the room on the sixth floor? Wherever she had left it, she knew she would never go back to reclaim it. She would never go back there. Never.